A Zombie Apocalypse Love Story Novella

Creating A Future

Kate L. Mary

Twisted Press

Published by Twisted Press, LLC, an independently owned company.

One

oisture dripped down my back as I pulled my suitcase from the ferry with a huff, the wheels bumping onto the dock where I paused to look around. My arms ached and I was sweaty, not to mention exhausted after a long day of travel, and I couldn't wait to take a shower and change so I could have a glass of wine. I'd left my house at four o'clock in the morning to catch my flight, and it was well after five in the evening now. It had taken two planes, two taxis, and two ferries to get here, which seemed like a hell of a lot considering I wasn't the least bit excited.

Even so, I couldn't help admiring the view as I lugged my suitcase forward. The wheels thumping over the wooden dock was the only sound other than the lapping of the water against the shore, but I barely noticed, too distracted by my surroundings. The resort and marina were absolutely breathtaking. Situated on a hill, the hotel was majestic in its opulence, with an infinity pool to the left and a restaurant beside it that overlooked the crystal-clear water. Monohulls and catamarans and even a couple multi-million-dollar yachts bobbed in the water as I passed. The only thing on Scrub Island was the Resort, Marina, and a handful of vacation homes and villas—all of them way out of the price range for normal people—because no one actually lived here full time. Which was why it had taken so long to get here.

Only a handful of people were visible as I headed for the Dream Yacht Charters office. Not a lot, which was how the whole day had been. The flights half full, and the usually bustling Atlanta airport more like a ghost town. So many people had canceled their plans in light of everything going on, but not me. My family had begged me to, which still felt surreal after two years of them harping on me to get on with my life, but I'd refused to stay home. I needed this, even if I still didn't know what *this* would turn out to be. If nothing else, it would be a break or a way to clear my head. At least that was what I kept telling myself.

The office was easy enough to find, and after checking in, I followed the instructions the woman behind the desk had given me, winding my way between boats in search of the correct one. I didn't know a whole lot about boats and had never sailed personally but I'd been given the basic information when I booked the trip. It was a sixty-two-foot catamaran—meaning it had two hulls instead of one—and could accommodate twelve passengers, including the crew. The rooms would be small, but I didn't care as long as it got me away from home for a while, and from the pictures I'd seen, I knew the views would be incredible. Crystal blue water and plenty of island fun, plus snorkeling and who knew what else. I could get a tan and relax, and if all went well, I'd return home feeling more like my old self.

I stopped when I reached the boat, craning my neck to catch a glimpse of the name to make certain I was in the right place. My long dark hair, sticky with sweat, fell over my face and I pushed it aside, holding it back so I could see. The words *Suzie Dear* were scrawled across the hull of the boat, confirming I'd reached my destination, and I let out a long breath. I was desperate to shower, change, and grab a drink—maybe even some food.

"Hello?" I called almost hesitantly.

The boat bobbed lazily on the water as I waited for someone to come out and help me, but a few seconds passed, but no one appeared. I twisted my hair around my hand and exhaled, silently wishing I'd thought to carry a hair tie. When a minute passed and still no one came, I studied the boat, trying to decide if I would be able to climb aboard without ending up in the water.

It was tied to the dock, but there were several inches of space and a lot of room for error. Especially when it came to someone like me who'd never set foot on a yacht in her life. Still, I thought I might be able to make it if I left my suitcase where it was. Hopefully, anyway.

I took a deep breath and reached out, grabbing the railing at the back so I could haul myself forward. Just as I did, the whole thing shifted, and I clung tighter to the rail as I made the jump. The boat rocked when I landed, but I was secure thanks to my grip, and I only stayed where I was for a few seconds before climbing the two steps.

A sitting and dining area stood in front of me, and I could see the interior through the glass door. All the lights were on, illuminating the kitchen and another seating area, but the door was shut, telling me the air conditioning was running.

We left the marina the next morning, so I doubted I was the first person to show up, but if anyone else was here, they were either below deck or off enjoying the resort because no one was in sight. Not even the crew. Which was beyond frustrating. I was filthy and tired, and I wanted to get settled in and cleaned up, but I had no clue what to do.

I looked around, hoping to spot someone who worked for the charter company or even the marina, but the dock was deserted. The seconds ticked by, and I shuffled from foot to foot, uncertain what I should do. Wait or go in?

After a few more seconds, I pulled the sliding glass door open a crack. Cool air rushed out, and I paused to listen. Nothing.

"Hello?" I called but was once again greeted by silence.

Glancing back to where my suitcase sat, I tried to decide what to do. I hadn't expected to have to navigate this situation on my own since the woman in the office had said someone would be here to greet me, but by this point, it was obvious no one was on the boat. I could wander around—maybe they had names on the doors—or wait and hope someone showed up. In my exhaustion, both options were irritating, but since the second one was doubly annoying, I decided to just go for it.

I stepped inside and once again called out, "Hello? Is anyone here?"

The kitchen stood in front of me, complete with double sinks, a cooktop, and an oven, as well as a seating area. A staircase heading into the bowels of the boat stood in each of the four corners of the room, which I knew led to the staterooms. I walked to the nearest one, pausing at the top of the stairs to listen, but headed down when I once again heard nothing. The hallway below was dark and narrow, but the bedroom door stood open, revealing a bed covered in a burgundy blanket. White towels that had been twisted into swans sat in the middle, and the sight momentarily distracted me as I recalled the trip to Punta Cana Michael and I had taken four years ago. I'd been so ecstatic when we'd stepped into our room to find swans just like these on our bed.

Pushing the memory down, I turned my attention to the door. Just like I'd thought, a piece of paper had been taped there, two names printed on it in a bold font.

Robert and Sylvia Miller

I headed back up, moving across the kitchen to another set of steps.

This hall was identical to the one I'd just left, but here nothing had been taped to the door. Peering inside, I instantly realized why. Instead of one bed, there were two. Bunkbeds. This room must have been for the crew.

Once again, I headed up, this time crossing to the set of stairs in the nearest corner of the room. Apparently, the third time really was the charm, because the name on this door was the one I'd been looking for.

Moira Rushing.

The bed was made up just like the first one, and beyond that was a small bathroom that gave me claustrophobia just looking at it. I'd known before arriving that the rooms would be tiny but knowing and seeing were two different things.

Why was I here again?

For a moment, I couldn't remember, then all my family's nagging came screaming back and I cringed. For two years I'd been moping, and for two years they'd been telling me to move on. It wasn't like I hadn't wanted to, it was just that the idea had exhausted me. Almost as much as the constant lectures. I'd still been reeling from the most recent *move-on-with-your-life* speech my mom had given me when a co-worker started showing off pictures of her parents' sailing trip to the BVIs, and in my fragile state, it had seemed like a sign. I'd booked the trip that day, finally spending some of the money I'd been sitting on for so long. My parents had thought I was insane, which had only made me more irritated. *They* were the ones who'd told me to go out and do something, who'd suggested a change of scenery, and yet they'd acted like I'd sold everything I owned so I could move halfway across the world, not booked myself a luxury vacation.

I was starting to think making them happy was an impossible feat.

Sighing, I turned my back on my room and headed up the stairs. Now that I knew where my cabin was, I needed to figure out how to get my suitcase onto the boat.

Just as I reached the top of the steps, I slammed into an object so firm it felt like a wall.

"Whoa!" The man I'd bumped into grabbed my shoulders like he was keeping me on my feet.

"Oh my God." I put my hand to my heart, which felt like it was going to explode from the shock of literally running into this man. "You scared me."

"Sorry." He released me and stepped back, a crooked smile on his face as he waved to the suitcase sitting at his side. *My* suitcase. "I take it this is yours."

"Yeah. Thanks." I shoved my hair out of my face, cringing at the way it stuck to the back of my neck. "Sorry to just wander around. No one was here to help."

His smile widened, and it suddenly hit me just how attractive he was, which only seemed to emphasize how sweaty my skin was. I probably smelled like I hadn't showered in days.

"Not a big deal," he said, giving me a crooked smile that accentuated the dimple in his left cheek.

The overhead lights shone off he blond highlights in his shaggy brown hair as he shoved his hand through it. They were from the sun, as was his bronzed skin. He was dressed casually, wearing tan shorts and a white button-down shirt, the sleeves rolled up to the elbows. Nothing about him seemed to indicate that he was an employee, but since he didn't seem to have any luggage with him, I wasn't sure if he was a guest, either. Maybe his suitcase was already in his room?

"Are you a guest?" I asked, taking a step back to put distance between us.

Would this guy be on the boat the whole week? God, I hoped not. He was too good-looking, and I'd come here to get my mind on something other than attractive men who had the ability to smash a vulnerable woman's heart into a million pieces.

"Captain," he replied, his crooked smile growing as he looked me up and down, making the hair on my scalp tingle. "Although, not your captain. Sadly."

"Oh," was the only thing I had time to say before the sliding glass door opened, pulling my attention that way.

The Adonis in front of me turned as another man stepped inside. "You have a passenger!"

"That so," the second man said.

Thankfully, this guy was well into his fifties and

not least bit attractive. He had a weathered look about him that told me he'd been working in the sun for years, his chin was dotted with gray stubble, and he had a long, gray ponytail that went to the middle of his back.

"Sorry for not being here to greet you," he said, tilting the hat perched on his head and offering me a friendly smile. "It's been a crazy day. Lots of cancelations and all that. To be honest, I wasn't sure if we were going to get anyone."

"Oh." I looked around, suddenly worried the whole trip would be canceled and I was going to have go home with my tail tucked between my legs.

"Not to worry," the gnarled man said. "We've got things under control now." He held his hand out. "Captain Dan at your service."

"Moira," I replied, taking his hand in mine. "Moira Rushing."

The captain pumped my hand twice in a firm grip that seemed at odds with his thin arms, nodding to the staircase at my back. "I take it you found your stateroom."

"I did." I dropped my arm to my side when he released my hand. "I was hoping to take a quick shower then grab something to eat. It's been a long day."

"Traveling to the island from the states is always an ordeal," the captain replied, and his blue eyes twinkled with his smile. "But I imagine it was twice as difficult with everything going on. Did you have any trouble?"

"No, no trouble." I shook my head, my mouth turning down as I thought about the nearly empty airports and half full flights. "Things in the US were a bit strange, and I was concerned the ferry and cab I'd reserved would be canceled, but everything went smoothly once I got to the Virgin Islands."

"We haven't really been affected just yet," the captain replied.

At his side, the other guy stood listening, his

hands shoved in his pockets as he leaned against the counter at his back, his hazel eyes intent on me. My scalp prickled under his gaze, making me even more thankful he wasn't going to be on my boat. I didn't need silly distractions in the form of an attractive guy who was only looking for a quick lay.

"Hopefully, all this will have blown over by the time I get back home."

I shifted when a strange feeling twisted in my stomach. Things had been shutting down when I left, stores restricting their hours and schools beginning to close to stop the spread of whatever this virus was, but the CDC was confident the changes would help. It was the only reason I hadn't canceled my trip. Despite how against me traveling outside the US my family had been. I was in the British Virgin Islands, though, and getting home would be easy. It wasn't like I'd gone to the Middle East.

The cell phone attached to Captain Dan's hip started vibrating, and he sighed when he pulled it free. "I need to take this," he said apologetically. "Get settled in and make yourself at home." He turned to face the other man as he accepted the call, the phone inches from his face when he said, "You'll give her the lay of the land for me, Boone?"

"No problem."

Captain Dan nodded once, then hurried outside, the phone now pressed against his ear. "What now?"

Once we were alone, Boone lifted my suitcase and headed for the stairs. "Let me show you how things work."

I followed him, ducking my head as I descended. The space was confining enough to give off the impression I would hit my head, but since the man in front of me had no issue, I knew it was an illusion. He was at least a head taller than me.

Boone stepped into my small room and set my suitcase on the floor at the end of the bed, but I was still in the hall. Both because I couldn't imagine a scenario where two people would fit into the cramped space and because I didn't want to get that close to him.

"There's a storage area under the bed for your suitcase." The guy didn't look at me as he lifted the mattress, revealing a space just big enough to fit my bag. He let it drop after a second and turned toward the bathroom. "The bathroom should be pretty self-explanatory except for maybe the toilet." His gaze darted to me. "Have you been on a sailboat before?"

"No." I was still in the hall, my head poking into the room and my neck craned so I could see what he was doing while still keeping my distance.

"The toilets run on saltwater, which helps with your water supply, so you have to fill the bowl by pushing this button first." He pressed a button and a motorized groan filled the room. After a second, he released it and turned back to me. "Toilet paper and other sanitary items go into the trashcan. We don't need those getting dumped in the ocean."

"Ocean?" I asked, suddenly alarmed.

He pressed his lips together, studying me for a second before saying, "We open the tanks when we're out to sea to empty the waste. They're closed when we're in the harbor, though. We don't want the trash in the ocean, so it's important to put the toilet paper in the trashcan. Got it?"

"Oh." My gaze went to the toilet. "That makes sense. I hadn't thought about it."

"Yeah, I'm sure most people wouldn't unless they've been on a boat." He turned back to the toilet. "Press this button to flush when you're done."

Again, a motorized groan filled the room, only this time, the water rushed from the toilet instead of into it.

"That should be all you need to know." Boone said when he was facing me again. "Captain Dan is experienced, so you don't need to worry about any other little details while you're out there. Questions?"

"No," I said.

"Good." Boone stepped from the room, crowding the hall, and I pressed my back against the wall. He grinned as if amused by my need to keep my distance. "Have fun out there, Moira."

"Thanks," I whispered.

He looked at me a second longer before chuckling softly. He was shaking his head when he climbed the stairs, leaving me alone.

Once he was gone, I finally stepped into my room. I imagined prison cells were bigger than this, and the irony wasn't lost on me. I just hoped the sights were enough to make up for the cramped space.

BY THE TIME I SLID INTO A CHAIR AT THE BAR——CLEAN and no longer sweaty—I was torn between wanting to drink all night and wanting to curl up in my impossibly small room and go to sleep. I'd thought this trip was a good idea, but now I couldn't imagine how I'd come to that conclusion. The parents of a co-worker I barely knew go sailing and somehow that meant I should? Yes, a room on a catamaran where I could rest and recharge while someone else did the sailing and cooking sounded amazing. But thinking about the tiny room that was supposed to be my refuge made me want to slap myself. Or take the next ferry out of here.

"What can I get you?" the man behind the bar asked, wiping his hands on a towel.

His Caribbean accent was thick, reminding me somewhat of the more commonly recognized Jamaican accent, but not quite matching it, and he had dark brown skin and eyes to match, which were soft and welcoming.

"Chardonnay please," I said. "And a menu."

He smiled, revealing straight white teeth and dimples in both cheeks. "Long day?"

"Just got here."

He nodded as he slid a menu onto the bar in front of me. "From the US?"

"Yes."

I was only half paying attention to him, my mind shifting gears as I scanned the menu, but I saw it when his smile faltered.

"How are things there?"

I'd been trying to ignore the weight in my stomach since boarding the plane this morning, but his words made it impossible. "Not awful." It was only a half lie. "They're getting things under control."

"Good." His shoulders relaxed as he grabbed a glass, as if my words had been a comfort to him, then he bent to get a bottle of wine from the fridge. When he stood, he said, "We're seeing a lot of strange things on the news, and the resort isn't as busy as usual."

He poured about twice as much wine into the glass as usual then scooted it to me.

"Thanks." I titled the glass toward him before taking a big gulp of the cold liquid. "I think it's being exaggerated on the news. I mean, they locked down the cities that are really bad. The area I'm from—Ohio—has barely been affected at this point."

"Let's hope you're right."

Again, the heaviness inside me seemed to grow, but I ignored it as I took another drink of wine. Everything was going to be okay. This trip would help me unwind, help me find myself, and when I returned home a week from now, things would be back to normal. Not just for me, but for everyone else as well. This virus wouldn't get the best of humanity. It couldn't.

I SLEPT WELL THAT NIGHT, THE BOAT BOBBING ON THE water only slightly since it was still in the marina, and woke early thanks to the sun shining in through my window. After dinner and three glasses of wine the night before, I'd returned to the boat and gone straight to bed without seeing anyone. Not even Captain Dan. We had hours before we'd be heading out, but it still seemed strange that no one else had shown up. When I'd booked this trip months ago, I'd managed to snag the last available cabin on the boat, but now I found myself wondering if anyone else would even be here.

My stomach rumbled as I slid out of bed. Once we left the harbor, food and coffee would be waiting for me every morning when I woke, but today I was responsible for my own meal. Not that I cared. I'd been too tired to give the resort more than a cursory glance the night before, and I was looking forward to getting a better look at the place.

Before heading out, I threw on a thin, white sundress and brushed my teeth and hair, twisting it into a loose knot on the top of my head. From what I understood about the trip, I'd be spending the majority of the next few days in a swimsuit, so I hadn't even bothered packing makeup. This was supposed to be a break for me, after all, which meant focusing on relaxing and not what I looked like.

The hotel and marina were twice as beautiful in the early morning light. Other people were out, and while most were employees, I passed a few tourists as well. I'd been given the option of sleeping on the boat the night before we left for a small fee, or staying at the resort, and I started to wonder if everyone else had chosen the hotel. It was over five hundred dollars a night for a basic room, and although I could have easily afforded it, I hadn't been interested in spending that much money for one night and had opted to go straight to the catamaran.

The top of the infinity pool came into view when I reached the second level, the early morning sun sparkling off the crystal blue water. The restaurant was just past it, the seating area outside covered by a thatched roof and overlooking the harbor and nearby island. The view was so breathtaking that I found myself slowing to enjoy it, and just like that, some of my unease melted away. Despite last night's uncertainty, I suddenly felt certain I'd made the right decision. Two years of licking my wounds was enough. It was time to recharge and move on.

After eating a veggie omelet and sucking down two mimosas, I headed back to the boat, more excited than ever to start my vacation. More people were on the docks now, and I returned the many smiles thrown my way. I lifted my hand to shield my eyes from the sun when *Suzie Dear* came into view. Captain Dan was behind the wheel—or whatever it was called—inputting information into what I assumed was the navigation system. I knew absolutely nothing about sailing and had given little consideration to the crew and what they'd be doing, and a sudden trepidation swept over me at the thought of being on a real sailboat. Would I be expected to help? Would I learn anything about how this boat worked?

"You're going to bump into me again," a teasing voice said, pulling me from my thoughts.

My gaze snapped to the dock in front of me where Boone had stopped in the middle of pulling a cart that reminded me of a wheelbarrow.

Heat warmed my cheeks, and I took a step back. "Sorry. I was admiring the boat."

"Getting excited to head out?" he asked, grinning.

"Yes. But a little nervous, too."

"Nothing to be nervous about. Captain Dan grew up sailing. You're in good hands."

"Oh." I let out a deep breath. "That's good. It suddenly occurred to me that I didn't really know what I was getting into. I mean, when I booked this trip, I was really just thinking of getting away for a while."

Boone's eyebrows rose in surprise. "You're here by yourself?"

"Yes."

A breeze blew, grabbing my skirt and lifting it slightly, and I didn't miss the way his eyes moved to my legs. I wasn't nearly as bronzed as the man in front of me, but a hint of summer tan remained, and my legs were toned and shapely. Exercise was one of the few things I hadn't given up two years ago when my heart got trampled, mainly because yoga had given me a chance to escape life and running had been an excuse to get out of the house when my parents were driving me crazy. Thankfully, I'd only had to stay with them for three months. There was nothing more frustrating—and humiliating—than having to move back home at the age of twenty-seven.

"That isn't very common," Boone said. "People coming on their own, I mean."

"I'm sure it isn't." I avoided his questioning gaze by once again focusing on the boat that would very soon whisk me out to sea. There were other people on the deck now. Other guests, I could only assume. "But I'm a loner and going places by myself doesn't bother me."

It was a lie. Not that I would ever admit it.

"It takes a secure person," Boone replied.

Once again, my focus moved to him. He'd set the cart down and was studying me intently, his hazel eyes more curious than they had been before. There was appreciation in them as he scanned my face, making me flush. Was it because I'd said I was okay being alone? The thought made me want to laugh. What a fraud I'd become over the last two years. What a pathetic, lonely, self-loathing person. Michael had been right. I *was* ridiculous.

I looked away from Boone, not wanting him to see the truth in my eyes.

After a second, he cleared his throat, and I watched out of the corner of my eye as he lifted the cart once again. "Have a good trip, Moira."

"Thank you." I headed off without glancing at him again.

On the boat, Captain Dan and a man with dark skin and long dreadlocks were getting things ready for our departure, their hard work contrasting with the laid-back air of the two older couples at the back of the boat. Cups of coffee in front of them, they were gathered around a table, smiling and chatting.

"You must be our lovely traveling companion," the woman closest to me said when I stepped onto the boat. "I'm Sylvia Miller, and this my husband Robert."

"Moira," I said, taking the woman's outstretched hand.

Sylvia's platinum blonde hair was cut to her chin in a dramatic bob, every strand smooth and perfectly placed. She was thin and well put together, and everything about her screamed money. Her husband, too, looked like the stereotypical wealthy older man, from his pressed khaki pants to his boat shoes. Like Sylvia, Robert offered me his hand, which I took without hesitating. He smiled, but studied me with interest, although nothing about the look made me uneasy.

"Bridge," the other woman said, holding her hand out as well. "Short for Bridget." She waved to the potbellied man at her side. "My husband, Reggie."

Like Sylvia and Robert, these two clearly had money—the three-carat rock on Bridge's ring finger told me that much—but they looked beachier and more relaxed. Bridge in a loose fitting coverup that was cut low, revealing just a glimpse of the black swimsuit beneath, and Reggie in a pair of bright, floral swim trunks and a t-shirt that said *Grand Cayman Islands*.

"So nice to meet you," I said, shaking hands with the second couple.

"We've been sitting here speculating about why a single woman in her twenties would book a trip like this," Sylvia said, getting right to the point as her sharp, blue eyes narrowed on me. "Now that I've seen you, I have to admit, I'm twice as curious."

"Just running from the law." I forced out a laugh

and waved my hand, trying to brush the question off as nothing even though my stomach had twisted into knots.

"Running from something, I'm sure," Bridge said, her expression knowing. "Not that you have to tell us. I've lived enough years to know that sometimes you just need a break to get a fresh outlook on life." The woman patted the seat beside her. "Sit down. Have some coffee. Enjoy yourself."

I could tell by her bright smile and the compassion in her eyes that she meant it. It was also clear that she was going to be a great ally when it came to Sylvia, whose eyes were sparkling with curiosity.

I slipped onto the bench at her side just as footsteps headed down the stairs. A second later, Captain Dan and the other man came into view.

"Morning everyone. We're just about ready to set off, but first I wanted to introduce my skipper to you." He waved to the man at his side, who was probably around thirty and had a smile as laid back and kind as Dan's. "John has been sailing as a skipper with Dream Yacht Charters for a few years now. He'll be doing the majority of the fishing and cooking, and he's here to answer any questions you might have along the way. I know the Millers and Swansons are old hats at this, but since it's Moira's first time, I wanted to make she knew who to go to." He paused to look us over. "Sound good?"

Heads bobbed, my own included, and Captain Dan's smile widened. "Good, good. I know you all have an itinerary, but I'm going let you know where we're headed every day anyway, as well as what to expect. The islands here are close together for the most part, but we'll still have a couple longer days of sailing, including today as we make our way to our first stop, which is Norman Island. We'll moor for the night there, but we'll have plenty of time before it gets dark to grab some dinner at Pirates Blight, then we can head over to Willy T's for drinks. Tomorrow, we can snorkel in the caves before heading out again." His smile widened. "Who knows, we might even find some pirate treasure!"

The two couples and John laughed, but since I had no clue what they were talking about, I could only smile. Not that it mattered. With each passing second, I was feeling more and more certain I'd made the right choice. This was going to be an adventure of a lifetime.

The catamaran rocked beneath my feet, moving with the gently lapping waves. The first few days on the boat I'd grabbed for the lifelines whenever it happened, but not anymore. I had my sea legs now.

A laugh broke out of me, but it was bitter and coated in tears that threaten to choke me, and I ended up having to close my eyes and swallow. I kept them shut, sucking salty air in through my nose before exhaling. Trying to find some kind of calm deep inside me. There was none, but that was to be expected considering everything that had happened.

When I opened my eyes, I instinctively looked over my shoulder, back toward the closed salon door as if I could see below deck to where the bodies sat rotting. Six of them. Six people I hadn't known two weeks ago who I now couldn't think about without sobbing. They were meant to be traveling companions while I found myself, then the virus reached our little bubble of paradise and changed everything. They had been my lifelines through all this. People to commiserate with while we went through our own personal nightmares that became inexplicably connected. Now they were gone, and like my family back in the states, I would never see their smiling faces again.

Their bodies, though, were still horribly present.

I shuddered involuntarily and wrapped my arms around myself like I was cold even though it had to be over ninety degrees. The sun was directly above me and beating down on my head with a punishing intensity that made me feel like I was on the verge of being baked. My skin was already tender to the touch—sunblock hadn't exactly been at the forefront of my mind over the last few days—and sticky. I felt gritty and greasy, and as much as I hated to dwell on it in the face of everything else, it was starting to get to me. How long had it been since I showered? Days. We stopped using the water for anything but drinking after John got too sick to help Captain Dan sail. Our freshwater tanks were limited, and without someone to get us to the next port, there would be no way to replenish the supply.

Conserving the water had only been a temporary solution and we'd known it. We'd known eventually we'd have to figure out a way to get more water, but it was something we'd decided to deal with when the time came. Which was where I now found myself. Except I was no longer part of a *we*. I was just *me*. Alone on a boat in the Caribbean and surrounded by water I couldn't drink with no way to get more.

I sank to the swim deck and my feet dropped into the water. It was cool and refreshing and crystal blue. So clear I could see ten, fifteen feet down. Below me, a long, dark form swam in a few lazy circles before moving under the boat and out of sight. A barracuda. They were common in the Caribbean and I'd seen dozens of them over the last two weeks. Too many to count. Not that I'd tried.

My gaze moved from the fish to the beach. Even though I wasn't sure if I could manage it, I knew what I needed to do. I had to get to shore and find water and supplies. We were moored maybe a hundred feet from the beach, which was roped off to prevent boats from getting too close. Both because the rocks jutted up, making it dangerous, and also so tourists could swim. I'd done it myself less than two weeks ago. We'd moored in this very spot and taken the dingy in as far as we could before swimming to shore. It had been one of my first few days on the boat, back when the beauty of this place had awed me to near speechlessness. It was still gorgeous, but now it felt like a mirage that had trapped me with promises it couldn't deliver.

The Baths sat to the left of the beach. The natural caves created from holes in the rocks and gaps between large boulders were one of the biggest attractions on Virgin Gorda, which could work to my advantage. A small bar was located on the next beach, which was reachable either through The Baths or by a trail. Farther up the island were two restaurants, and between the three places, I should be able to find some water. Food, too. It was less urgent than water, although still a concern. I hadn't eaten in more than twenty-four hours and even then, it had only been the last half of a granola bar.

My gaze moved to the dingy—a heavy-duty inflatable raft with a motor—and everything in me tightened. Two weeks on the water meant I had plenty of experience at this point, but it wasn't like I'd actually driven the thing. I was just a passenger on this boat. The crew had done all the heavy lifting, including driving the dingy to shore. Too bad figuring it out was my only option if I wanted to survive.

The dingy hung at the back of the boat, suspended more than five feet above the water, and I had no idea how to get it down. Why hadn't I thought to ask Dan or John how to do it before they got too sick? It had been stupid to put it away after we used it the last time, but none of us had really been thinking that far ahead. We'd all been too focused on Sylvia, who had been the first to come down with symptoms. And we'd been in shock, because until that moment, we'd thought we were safe. Thought the virus wouldn't be able to touch us.

What a joke.

I climbed to my feet and dragged myself to the back of the boat, eyeing the dingy like I suspected it was plotting to kill me. I'd have to turn the power on first, then find the right controls to lower it, then undo the hooks. I'd watched Dan do it a couple times, but that didn't mean I was confident in my ability to figure out all the necessary steps. Two weeks on the boat, and I still had no idea what half the mechanisms were called. Since John had been the third person to die, I'd helped Dan enough that I could at least assist someone who did know how to sail at this point. Too bad there wasn't anyone left. Not since Dan died yesterday.

Knowing what I had to do, I climbed the stairs to the helm and looked the controls over. It seemed pretty straightforward, but I still held my breath as I pressed the first button. The lights on the panel flickered, but the hum of the engine didn't follow. Good. I needed power but I didn't want to waste what little fuel we had.

Once I was sure the power to the right components had been turned on, I pressed a second button. A mechanical groan followed, and I let out a sigh of relief as the dingy slowly began to lower. It only took a couple minutes to reach the water, but even once it had, I didn't release the button. I needed some slack in the ropes to free the dingy.

I scooped up a waterproof backpack, which had a second bag stuffed inside, and tossed them into the small vessel, followed by a pair of flippers, a mask, and a snorkel. Then I tentatively climbed into the dingy. It rocked, throwing me off balance and forcing me to flop down so I didn't fall in the water. When I stood again, I made sure my feet were firmly planted. Undoing the hooks wasn't an easy task with the water pushing the dingy around, but I managed to get first one then other undone. It was a relief, but the hardest part was yet to come.

Perched on the side of the dingy, I lowered the engine, planted my feet for traction, and pulled on the rope. The motor made a sound but didn't turn over. While I'd never done this myself, I'd seen Captain Dan or John do it many times, and I knew I needed to adjust the choke. Once I had, I tried again. Still no luck. A little more adjusting and I gave the rope another pull, and the engine finally roared to life. I would have let out a whoop of triumph except I knew I wasn't out of the woods.

Driving a dingy was tricky because you had to move the tiller in the opposite direction you wanted to go, which was contrary to every instinct I had. I knew this, but still bumped into the back of the boat when I gave the engine some gas. I swore under my breath before turning the tiller, this time managing to head in the correct direction. I went slowly at first, not wanting to hit the boat again, but once I was far enough away that I was no longer worried I was going to crash, I gave the engine a little more gas.

Ours wasn't the only catamaran moored here, and I had to be careful as I maneuvered between the other boats. There were three, and even though they were spaced far enough apart that they wouldn't crash into one another when the tide shifted, it was still a challenge for a novice dingy driver.

All three had been here before us, but I hadn't seen a single sign of life aboard them for days. I knew what that meant, but that didn't stop me from craning my neck as I went by. The first and closest one gave away nothing about the fates of those on board, but the one after it revealed a grisly scene that made my stomach contort. A man, his lifeless body bloated from the sun, was sprawled out on the deck, arms splayed at his sides and blank eyes staring up at nothing. I shuddered and looked away.

I avoided looking at the other boats after that. They were too far away and faced the wrong direction for me to get a good look anyway, or at least that was what I told myself. In truth, I just couldn't stomach it.

The wind blew just as I reached the roped off bathing area, carrying with it the stink of death. My stomach lurched, but I knew vomiting would be impossible. I was on empty.

I sat for a moment after killing the motor, staring at the shore. No one was around, and part of me wanted to just drive the dingy all the way to the beach. I knew getting back out to sea by myself would be next to impossible, though. We'd done it at different beaches during the first few days, and it had taken several of us to get the little boat off the beach and over the waves. Doing it on my own wouldn't work. Which meant swimming was my only option.

I wasn't scared of the water or the possibility of sharks. I'd made this trip once already and it had been fine—plus I hadn't seen a single shark since arriving here. It was getting my supplies back to the dingy that worried me. I had my waterproof backpack—courtesy of the captain—and the extra bag, which I'd have to drag behind me. It was a lot to carry any time, but especially considering I was exhausted and hungry, and I'd be swimming against the current.

Hopefully, I'd find some food and water on shore, and it would give me the energy I needed.

Knowing I didn't have a choice, I looped the dinghy's line around the rope bobbing on the surface of the water, then started my knot. Before this trip, I'd never even heard of a bowline knot let alone known how to tie one. I'd had enough practice since John's death, though, that I could now do it without much thought, and my fingers moved on their own, threading the line through the loop and around, then back through before pulling it tight, all the while my gaze on the distant shore. There was no movement, no sign of people. Not even leftover footprints in the sand. They'd all been washed away by the high tide, as if nature was already trying to forget that humans had ever tread here.

The thought sent a shudder down my spine.

Once I was sure the boat wouldn't float away, I grabbed my supplies. Flippers on and backpack secure, I took a deep breath and slipped into the water. It was cool and refreshing, and clear enough that I didn't necessarily need a mask to see what was below me. I had it on though, and I breathed through the snorkel as I swam, pumping my legs and using the flippers to propel me toward shore. Rocks and coral and sea anemones dotted the ocean floor, and brightly colored fish swam between them, oblivious to the decimated world above. The last time I was here, I'd spent nearly an hour swimming around, studying the fish and rocks in wonder. Now, though, I barely noticed them. It was crazy how much could change in such a short time.

I reached land and pulled myself to my feet, pausing to yank my flippers off. The sand here was different than other places I'd been. Softer. I wasn't sure if it was because Virgin Gorda was a volcanic island or if there was some other reason, I just knew it felt like I was walking on extra plush carpet, and it tried to suck me in with each step. It also made my trek more difficult, which irritated me since I was already exhausted.

I tossed my snorkel gear under a nearby tree and slipped the backpack off so I could wring out my hair. In the distance, my boat bobbed with the waves, nearly in sync with the others around it, but beyond that, the ocean was empty. No sailboats, no yachts, no ferries carrying passengers to jobs or vacation destinations. Other islands loomed in the distance, mountainous and beautiful and totally out of reach, but the world had gone silent.

I turned my back to them before I burst into tears.

The straps of my backpack dug into my shoulders when I slipped it back on, but I barely noticed. I was wearing only a swimsuit, but after two weeks on the boat, I'd gotten used to going around barely clothed. It was the only way to survive, especially once we'd had to stop running the air conditioning at night.

I shuddered again, thinking about the bodies on the boat and how hot it was, and how bad things were going to get. I had to formulate a plan. Had to figure out what to do either with them or with myself. Had to figure out how I was going to survive, or if it was even worth it.

But first, I needed water.

The trek through The Baths was longer and more tedious than if I used the trails, but it was more direct as well and it would keep me out of the sun, so I headed that way.

It was low tide, and the water wasn't as deep when I reached the first cave as it had been last time I was here. The opening was partially formed by boulders, but there was also a natural gap in the larger rocks that made an arch and led into other cave-like areas. I followed the same trail I had before, wading through water and climbing over rocks or squeezing through narrow openings, only now I was alone. Last time it hadn't just been my companions in the caves, but dozens of other travelers as well. A cruise ship had even docked on the island, and nearly a hundred people had spilled off the boat and filled The Baths, making them claustrophobic. Their voices had bounced off the surrounding rocks until I'd wanted to scream, but now I longed for the noise and people. For anything other than nothingness, really. It was entirely too silent for my liking.

Stairs had been constructed in places, allowing people to make it through the more treacherous areas more easily, and there were even two places where ropes had been placed to make climbing down easier. It had seemed fun my first time here—an adventure— but now it made me wish I'd hiked the trails instead.

Since I was more than halfway through, I trudged on.

I paused when I emerged from the caves, still half-expecting to find people even though logic told me I wouldn't. Like everything else, the beach was deserted, and while there were a few boats moored in the distance, they looked as lifeless as the ones I'd passed on my way to shore.

Last time I was here, there had been a long line of people waiting to order drinks at the bar. Now, though, it was closed. I headed that way, anyway.

When I reached the bar, I felt like smacking myself. It was locked. Of course, it was. Had I really thought I'd arrive to find it open and waiting, the ingredients laid out so I could make myself a pain killer and forget all my problems? Stupid.

Even though I knew getting inside was a long shot, I studied the padlock. It looked sturdy enough, but the wooden door was thin. If I could find something to break it down, I should be able to get in. Although that was a long shot, too. The Baths were a national park, and I couldn't imagine I was going to find a sledgehammer just lying around.

"Shit," I muttered as I turned my back to the bar. "Maybe I'll have better luck at the restaurant."

I headed for the trail that would take me up to the restaurant and bar.

It was a short walk, although the hot sun and my dry mouth made it feel twice as long, and soon buildings came into view. The park bathrooms and ticket office were to the right, but I headed left, which was where the restaurant sat.

When the pay showers came into view, I let out a groan. I'd completely forgotten they existed and seeing them made me wish I'd grabbed a few bucks before leaving the boat. Rinsing off with fresh water sounded amazing right now.

The sparkling water of the small pool beside the restaurant came into view, but my focus was on the dining area and bar beyond. Mercifully, it was open air, which meant I could walk right in, but I didn't even make it past the pool before I froze.

Someone was here.

A man sat under the shade of the overhang, his back to me as he stared out over the ocean. He had a glass in front of him and a plate of food, as well as an open bottle of rum. From this angle, I couldn't get a good look at his face, but there wasn't a streak of gray in his shaggy brown hair, and his broad shoulders hinted at youthfulness and strength. His skin was bronzed from the sun, but still light, telling me he probably wasn't local. At least not originally. Was he stranded here like me?

I scanned the area, but no one else was in sight. He was alone, like me, and while my heart leapt at the thought of having someone to help me, common sense told me to be cautious. I didn't know anything about him, and I was smart enough to realize that some people were dangerous. Doubly so now that law and order was as extinct as the dodo bird.

Still, I only paused for a few more seconds before forcing myself to move. I'd stay alert, but I had to talk to him. There was no other option. I had no idea what I'd do if I didn't find someone who could help me, because I wasn't just stranded in another country, I was trapped in a lifestyle I knew nothing about.

My feet scraped against the ground after three steps and his back stiffened. He spun to face me, nearly knocking the bottle of rum over in the process, and we both froze.

"You," he said just as I mumbled, "I know you."

It only took a moment to remember who he was. Two weeks had passed since we met on Scrub Island, and so much had happened that it felt like a different life, but he'd left an impression on me even though we'd barely spoken. Boone. The guy who'd helped me get my bags on the boat. I'd hadn't I'd never see him again even before the virus changed everything. I'd thought he and I were nothing but two people passing one another, never meant to meet again.

It seemed, however, I'd been wrong.

Feeling more confident now that I at least recognized the guy, I continued my trek around the pool. He watched me the whole time, his hazel eyes bloodshot and slightly hazy, but focused on my face. He'd grown a beard since the last time I saw him, but it wasn't what drew my attention. It was the expression in his eyes. The way he looked at me, the utter shock and preoccupation, told me he'd been as terrified of being alone as I was.

When I reached his table, I slid my backpack off and dropped it to the ground before taking a seat. I hadn't noticed the pitcher of ice water sitting in front of him before, but seeing it made my mouth fill with saliva.

I nodded toward it. "Can I?"

His head dipped once.

I grabbed the pitcher, not caring that there were no glasses, and lifted it to my lips. I sucked the cold water down, nearly choking in my desperation. It dripped from the sides of my mouth and onto my chest, cooling my hot skin, but I didn't stop. I gulped mouthful after mouthful until I couldn't breathe, then paused long enough to suck in a deep breath before drinking more. By the time I finished, there was a dull ache in my temples from the cold, but I couldn't care because my throat was no longer parched, and my stomach felt full and satisfied with its chilly contents.

Boone lifted his eyebrows in a slightly mirthful look, but his lips didn't pull up into a smile. "Thirsty?"

"We ran out of water on our boat," I said, and let out a long breath as the reality of it all swirled around me. "Everyone was sick, so I couldn't come ashore. Until now. It's just me. I'm all that's left."

Boone winced when I told him everyone was dead, and it hit me that he'd actually known both Captain Dan and John. More than I had, anyway. I should have been more sensitive.

"You don't have a desalinator on your boat?" he asked instead of bringing up the callous way I'd told him his friends—assuming they had been friends— were dead.

"I don't know what that is," I said even though the name gave its use away.

"It treats saltwater, so you can drink it. A big boat like yours should have one," he replied with a shrug. "Unless the owners cheaped out."

"Captain Dan never mentioned it," I said, mimicking his shrug.

"Stupid," he muttered as he lifted his glass to his lips, the brown liquid sloshing around.

I watched him throw the rum back, his eyes on me the whole time. His glass was empty when he set it down, and he reached for the bottle without so much as a word. His movements were slow but not relaxed. He was in shock, probably. I knew the feeling.

"What about you?" I asked when he said nothing.

"Me?" He lifted his eyebrows as he raised the glass again.

"Your boat, I mean. Your passengers and crew."

"Dead." He threw back more rum, wincing slightly like it burned. "Just like everyone else."

I looked around like someone would appear and prove him wrong, but nothing moved, and the only sounds were the distant roar of the ocean and the wind whipping a nearby flag through the air. The silence was unnerving.

Boone put his glass on the table and the sound echoed through the restaurant, making me jump.

When I turned back to face him, his intense hazel eyes were on me. "What happened to Dan and John?"

"They got sick." I let out a long breath, preparing to relive the horror of it all. "I'm sure it wasn't much different for you. We left Scrub Island and the first few days were great. We went to Norman Island and Willy T, then Peter Island. We stopped at another island and went snorkeling over that sunken ship."

"Salt Island," Boone said.

"Whatever." I shrugged to let him know the name didn't matter. "It was nice. Relaxing. Swimming and snorkeling and sailing. Sunshine. I'd almost forgotten about the virus. We came here next." I waved to the restaurant. "Moored on this side of the island then went to the other side the next day. That was where we were when heard travel in and out of the US had been suspended."

"I was on Anegada," Boone said.

"We never made it that far." I sank back, the weight of everything that had happened sweeping over me. "When we got back to the boat, Dan called Scrub Island and spoke with the office. They basically said they didn't know what to do. They also told us that people in Tortola had started coming down with the virus. We decided to stay on the boat, pool our money, and do our best to stay secluded. We hoped we could ride the whole thing out, you know?"

"We did the same," Boone said. "The company didn't tell us outright that it was okay, but they didn't tell anyone they had to come back immediately either."

"That was what Dan said." I let out a long breath. "We did okay for the next three days. We sailed around, avoided people as much as possible, and tried our best not to worry. Then Sylvia—Mrs. Miller—got sick. Things went fast after that. Robert, John, and Reggie were sick before Sylvia died, and by that point Bridge had started showing symptoms. They were all dead within forty-eight hours. Dan was the last holdout, but exposure was unavoidable in such close quarters." I looked down. "He died last night."

"That's pretty much how it went for us," Boone said. "Although, it's been almost two days since the last person on my boat died. That's why I'm here. I couldn't stand staying on that boat."

"Tell me about it," I muttered, still looking at my hands.

"What about you?"

I looked up, not sure what he was getting at. "Me?"

"Are you showing any symptoms?"

"No. Nothing. I'm exhausted and hungry—we're out of food, too—and thirsty, but that's it. It can't last, though. Right? I mean, I'm going to get it, too. I have to."

Boone pushed his plate toward me, and without thinking, I pulled it closer. There were some fresh veggies—lettuce and tomatoes and cucumbers—and some grilled fish. Mahi Mahi, I was pretty sure. I picked up a piece of white, flaky meat with my fingers and popped it into my mouth.

"I've heard some people are immune," Boone said.

I lifted my eyebrows as I chewed. "Immune?"

"That's the rumor." His shoulders rose and fell. "When there were people around to spread rumors, that is."

"It seems a little far-fetched, but what do I know."

I picked at the food, knowing I needed to eat but not having much of an appetite. The fish wasn't warm, but the flavor was still good, and despite the fact that it felt like rocks in my stomach, I was grateful for it.

Boone said nothing as I ate, nursing a glass of rum, his gaze on me but his hazel eyes devoid of any emotion that would allow me to guess what he might be thinking. I didn't know him, had only interacted with him a little, but he seemed like a different person than the one who'd showed me around the boat only two weeks ago. Then again, if I did manage to make it home somehow, I would probably seem like a stranger to my family. Nursing people as they died did that to a person.

The last bit of fish was in my mouth, and it turned to dirt at the memory of everything that had happened over the last few days. I swallowed anyway, although with great difficulty, then pushed the plate away as I once again lifted the pitcher of ice water to my mouth and began to drink.

It wasn't until I'd set it back down and the cubes clinked against the glass that I wondered why there was ice. Looking toward the bar, I noted the dark lights and still fans. The electricity had to be off, so where had the ice come from?

"How do you have ice?" I asked, my gaze moving back to Boone.

His shoulders rose and fell even as he explained. "The power was still on when I got here, but it finally went out this morning. Not all the ice has melted yet."

I stood, pushing the chair back. "Then I guess I should get some while I can."

Boone's head bobbed as he once again took a sip of rum.

Pitcher in hand, I headed to the back of the restaurant, only realizing once I'd reached the bar that the door to the kitchen had been broken open. Pausing, I glanced over my shoulder to where Boone still sat. His gaze had moved so he was once again staring at the distant ocean, but from inside the restaurant, I couldn't see what he was looking at. Nothing, probably. That was all that remained, after all. Nothing but the two of us and an emptiness that felt never ending.

The kitchen was dark, but there was light streaming in through both this door and the one at the back. It illuminated the now useless kitchen equipment. The two industrial ovens, fryers, and refrigerators. The door to the ice machine was hanging open, making me frown at how short-sighted Boone had been. If he'd shut it, he could have kept the ice longer. Either he hadn't been thinking that far ahead, or he'd assumed it wouldn't matter since he was on his own. I know I hadn't expected to find anyone here. Things had been too silent.

The ice was mostly melted at this point, but I was only half thinking about the cold water as I used the scoop to fill my pitcher. I had help. Relief washed over me as I thought about what that might mean. Before, I'd felt stranded. Trapped on a boat with rotting bodies and no way to escape. Now, though, I had a way out. Boone knew how to sail, which meant he could get us to another island and, if we were lucky, find a way back to the states. Things had to be better there. Didn't they? It was America, after all. If anyone could survive this thing, it was the United States.

It was what I'd been telling myself for the past two days even though I hadn't been able to get through to my family for over a week.

Dread filled me as I thought about the last conversation I'd had with my mom, and not wanting to be alone, I scooped up the icy water faster. Once the pitcher was full, I grabbed myself a glass and hurried back out to the restaurant, desperate to be with another person. The sight of the empty table, however, made me freeze. Where had Boone gone?

For a moment, I found myself wondering if I'd made him up. Had I so desperately wanted to find help that my mind had generated this mirage? No. The empty plate on the table told me he was real, but the missing glass and bottle of rum still had me doubting myself as I walked on.

Boone didn't come into sight until I'd reached the table, and when he finally did, I let out a sigh of relief. He was in the pool, glass in hand as he leaned against the wall, watching me approach.

"What are you doing?" I asked as I lowered myself to the ground next to the pool.

"It's hot." His shoulders lifted slightly as he sipped his rum, his gaze intent on me and less blank than before. "I'm sure you could use a dip, too."

My thoughts went back to the day we'd met. To the sweaty mess I'd been after traveling all day and how self-conscious I'd been when talking to Boone. What I wouldn't do to go back and have those problems again. Had I seriously thought going for twelve hours without a shower was a big deal? Even worse were the two years I spent nursing a broken heart, not willing to accept the fact that I was lucky. Lucky the asshole had left me when he did, giving me a chance to move on with my life. A chance I'd wasted.

The glass I'd taken from the bar was empty when I slipped into the pool, and even though my throat was still dry, I ignored the pitcher of icy water and waded over to where Boone leaned against the wall.

"Give me a drink," I said, holding the glass out to him.

His eyebrows rose in silent questions, but he complied without comment, pouring an inch of the brown liquid into the glass. I'd never been much of a rum drinker, but I didn't hesitate to throw the stuff back in one gulp. It burned, but only slightly, and I let out a little cough as I held the glass out a second time.

"More," I said in a raspy voice.

This time, Boone smiled.

"What are we drinking to?" he asked as he poured first more for me, then more for himself.

"Is there anything to drink to?" I replied, staring into my glass.

"We're alive," he said. "That's something."

"But we're stuck here." I looked up, the rum forgotten. "I mean, we are stuck here, right? Is it even possible to sail back to the states?"

"It's possible, although not likely." He took a drink, and I did the same, sipping it this time. "I mean, we could go from island to island as we work our way up. Puerto Rico to the Dominican Republic, Cuba, then the Bahamas, and then up Florida. The problem would be finding the supplies we need in each port. Then there's hurricane season."

Again, Boone downed some rum, but he seemed to be thinking it through. I waited, hope building in me as I sipped my own drink. There had to be a way. I just knew it. At that moment, as the silence stretched out, I felt as if I'd run into Boone for a reason. Fate or destiny, or something else. He would know how to get me home.

"Where are you from?" he asked after a prolonged silence.

"Ohio."

Boone frowned.

"But does that even matter? I mean, all we'll have to do is get to Florida, then we can go wherever we want. We're US Citizens, after all. The travel ban doesn't apply to citizens going back into the country."

"There's more to it than that."

Fear gripped me, squeezing my insides. "What do you mean?"

"They didn't just suspend travel going in and out of the US." Boone's gaze was on me, his words slow like he wanted to brace the impact of what he was about to say. "They've declared marshal law. Limited travel to everyone. Right now, you can't even go from state to state without prior approval."

My mom hadn't said anything about that. Had she? I thought back to that conversation, now more than a week and a half ago. I'd had to borrow a phone from Bridge since I hadn't set mine up to make international calls, but I'd gotten through. Mom had been sick, and so had my dad. My brother, too, but not my sister yet or the kids. The hospitals were full, according to Mom, that much I remembered. But she hadn't said anything about marshal law. She'd just told me to stay where I was and avoid people. She'd told me she loved me.

"Who told you travel in the US is suspended, too?" I whispered.

Boone's mouth turned down. "It was on the news."

He nodded toward the bar and I turned, following his gaze. There was a television mounted behind it, its screen dark just like everything else.

"It was still working when I got here, although that didn't last long," Boone said, his voice sounding suddenly far off. "A pre-recorded story from at least a week ago played on repeat, but I couldn't stop watching it. It was all I did my first day here. What's happening isn't confined to the BVIs. It's everywhere, Moira."

It was the first time he'd said my name, and it gave me a start. I didn't even know why.

I turned back to face him. "Tell me everything you know."

"The government lied or exaggerated the hold they had on this thing," he said, shaking his head, "I don't know which. I just know there's no stopping it."

No stopping it.

I felt like I'd left my body. It was something I'd heard people say before, but I had never understood it until this moment. I was weightless, floating above myself, feeling detached not just from who I was, but from the world around me. It couldn't be real. There couldn't really be a virus sweeping the world. It was a dream. I'd wake up tomorrow at home and everything would be okay.

"Moira?"

Hands touched my arms and I forced myself to focus. Boone had set his glass down and was leading me to the side of the pool, an expression of concern on his face. Was he worried about me? Should he be?

Boone helped me out and led me to a nearby lounge chair, urging me to lie down. I did, stretching out on my back, my gaze on the cloudless blue sky as he hurried away. He was back in no time, the pitcher of water and an empty glass in his hands. He poured me some of the cool liquid, sat at my side, and held it out to me.

"Drink."

I sat up and obeyed, gulping the water down so fast it got caught in my throat, making me cough. Boone patted my back. My eyes were stinging. Not from the water I'd choked on. From tears. They were burning my eyes, collecting, then spilling over when I blinked. Sobs followed, shaking my shoulders, and then I found myself in Boone's arms, my head against his bare chest, his skin warm against mine. He was whispering in my ear. Words of comfort. Over and over.

"It's okay. You're going to be okay. We're going to be okay. I promise."

How could he promise that?

I cried harder.

His arms tightened around me and he went silent, allowing me to sob as he held me. No longer trying to comfort me, but instead just being there. It was exactly what I needed. Comfort from another person. The knowledge that I wasn't alone in this world, that there were still other people out there. That we could somehow, against seemingly endless odds, create something out of the ruins of this world.

I prayed it was true.

I was sniffling when I finally pulled away, and Boone's bare chest—firm and tan—was damp from my tears and probably a little snot as well. It was something that would have humiliated me in the past, but in light of everything else going on, I couldn't make myself care. Not even a little.

I wiped my eyes with the heel of my hand and swallowed, trying to find my voice. "What now?"

Sunlight shimmered off the moisture in Boone's eyes when they met mine. "We need to figure out if there are other survivors somewhere. On another island, maybe. Tortola would be our best bet, but even here, on Virgin Gorda, there could be someone." His gaze moved past me to the road, his lips pressed together. "I haven't seen anyone, but maybe if we sail to the other side of the island."

"And if we don't find anyone?" I asked, voicing the worry that had been nagging at me. "What if we're all that's left?"

Boone's hazel eyes moved back to me. "We keep looking. There are so many islands to check. There have to be others. Either way, we need to gather supplies. Water and any food we can. Starting here."

He got to his feet, his hand grabbing mine almost as an afterthought and pulling me up with him. He was still holding it when he headed toward the kitchen.

"The electricity hasn't been out long, which means the food in the freezers should still be good." His gaze darted to me. "My catamaran has some solar panels that will help keep the fridge going, as well as allow us to use the power winch. There's no way to get those sails up without it. The boat is too big. It isn't enough to run the engines and electricity, but as long as we have wind, we can travel without having to worry about refueling." Boone glanced my way as we reached the kitchen, shaking his head slightly. "You can't sail. I forgot."

"I'm not an experienced sailor like you, but I can help a little bit." I shrugged, feeling useless but wanting him to know I could at least follow orders. "After John died and everyone else got sick, Dan needed help. He told me what to do, and I did it."

"Good." In the kitchen, Boone paused to look around, then glanced back at me. "I saw you brought a backpack."

"There's another bag inside, so I have two."

"That will be helpful."

He exhaled and ran his hand down his face, suddenly looking exhausted and overwhelmed, which was something that scared me. Of the two of us, he was the more capable one. If he felt overwhelmed, I was in deep shit.

My hand was still in Boone's, and he released it without seeming to notice he'd ever been holding it and headed toward the fridge.

He yanked the doors open and said, "We're kind of limited on what we're going to be able to take back to the boat since we have to snorkel there."

I thought of my flippers, discarded on the first beach, and wondered where Boone had left his things. He had a bag thrown over his shoulder, but no snorkel gear and I hadn't seen anything on the beach I'd swam to, but it was possible I'd missed it.

"Where's your boat?"

Boone paused in the middle of scanning the freezer's contents, so he could look my way. "I'm moored by the Baths. The beach where the little bar is."

"I'm at the other beach."

"No big deal." He'd turned his focus back to the fridge and was pulling things off the shelves, setting them on a nearby counter. "We only need one boat, anyway. You're on a 620 Lagoon, right?"

"I don't know." My shoulders rose and fell. "The name of the boat is *Suzie Dear*."

"That's the 620 Lagoon." He set a couple heads of lettuce down, then went for more. "It's the biggest Dream Yacht has, but the one I have is better. We'll take it. It's a little smaller, but it has more features that will help in a non-electricity situation."

"But my things."

The thought of not going back to the boat, of leaving all my personal items behind, sent fear shooting through me. That was like accepting I would never again need my passport or credit cards. That my driver's license was useless. That my cell phone, which was currently dead, would stay that way forever.

As if sensing my trepidation, Boone stopped what he was doing and turned to face me. "It's okay. We can sail over and get your stuff. It's the opposite direction from where we want to go, but we have a lot of daylight left, so I'm not worried."

I relaxed, let out a sigh, and gave him a grateful smile.

It melted away a second later when I thought of another issue. "My snorkel gear is on that beach. I didn't want to drag it with me through the Baths, so I left it there."

Boone pressed his lips together, his thoughtful gaze moving past me. "There's a giftshop over there. I haven't been inside in years, but I bet we can grab some gear there. It will probably be nicer than what you borrowed from the company, anyway."

My shoulders relaxed. "Okay. That sounds good."

Boone gave a firm nod and went back to digging through the fridge, reminding me why we were here. I couldn't sail or navigate my way from island to island, but that didn't mean there weren't other things I could do to help.

"I'm going to grab my bags," I said, then darted out of the kitchen.

My things were right where I'd left them, and I

scooped them up and turned on my heel, ready to head back, but froze before taking a single step.

Was I seeing things?

Virgin Gorda was tall and rocky, and we were at a high point that looked down over huge boulders to the ocean. From here, I could see several sailboats—both monohulls and catamarans—bobbing on the water. They were far away, making it difficult to get a really good look at them, but I could have sworn I'd spotted a figure on one. It had only been in sight for a moment, but it had looked like a person stumbling around on the deck. Was it wishful thinking, or were there other people out there, immune like Boone and me?

I waited a second longer, squinting into the distance, then shook my head and turned away when nothing appeared. If someone was out there, we'd see them when we sailed by in a little bit. There was nothing I could do about it from all the way up here, though.

I KICKED MY LEGS AS HARD AS I COULD, WORKING against the current trying to push me back to shore. Boone had been right about the giftshop, and as a result, I was sporting brand new snorkel gear. With the heavy bag strapped to my back and another two gripped in each hand, the flippers didn't seem to be helping much. They flapped through the water as I moved my legs, my focus on the rocky ocean floor in hopes that I could block out the burning ache in my calves. Colorful fish effortlessly swam between rocks and coral as if mocking me, and I kicked harder. A wave lifted my body, trying to force me back, and I put more effort into my kicks. Right, left, right, left.

Boone was in front of me, about seven feet of space between us. He was carrying just as many bags, but his were loaded down the heavier items. Some cans and jars of food, and bottles of water. We'd be able to refill them on the boat since apparently his had a water maker, so we hadn't taken a lot, but we were hoping to get more on another island. One we'd be able to drive the dingy right up to rather than have to snorkel to.

I lifted my head as I continued swimming and was relieved to see that we were more than halfway to our destination. The little gray dingy bobbing less than ten feet in front of us felt like a lifeline after the exhausting swim and overly emotional day, and I couldn't wait to plop down inside it. Of course, I knew the hardest part would be pulling myself out of the water. It required a lot of upper body strength, something I'd never really known I didn't have until this trip.

Lowering my face back into the water, I kept swimming.

I could tell when Boone reached the dingy, because he righted himself and lifted the bags out of the water. One by one they disappeared from sight, and Boone followed a second later, pulling himself up with ease. Kicking with every ounce of energy I had left, I cut through the water, finally stopping when the bottom of the boat was six inches in front of me.

Boone's face was hovering over me when I surfaced. "Pass me those bags."

His hand was out and waiting as I lifted first one then the other, then I wiggled out of the backpack and handed it to him. No longer weighed down, I let out a deep breath.

"Give me your hand," Boone said. "I can help."

Knowing I was too exhausted to get into the boat on my own, I gratefully took his outstretched hand. I kicked my legs while he pulled, and my body was propelled out of the water. The top of my skimpy swimsuit shifted in the process and my breasts spilled out, but I was on my stomach on the side of the dingy and told myself Boone hadn't seen anything. I also tried to convince myself it didn't matter. In light of everything else going on, flashing someone I barely knew shouldn't have been a very big concern.

I adjusted my top then flopped into the dingy, landing on the floor in a heap that wasn't at all graceful and hitting my knee on an oar in the process. Not that I cared what I looked like or that I was most definitely going to have a bruise. We were on the boat and soon we'd be on Boone's catamaran. Then we could go find help.

"You okay?" he asked, reaching down to help me.

"Yeah." I waved him off, twisted so I was on my butt, then pushed myself up.

He was already sitting to the left of the motor, propped on the edge of the dingy, so I moved to the right. Once I was perched across from him, he untied the boat, making certain the rope wasn't dangling in the water.

The motor roared to life on his first try, and I clung to the little handle as we started moving, cutting through the water and heading toward our destination. Thankful I wasn't the one driving the dingy this time.

"You make this look easy," I called, raising my voice so I could be heard over the motorized hum and splashing water.

"I've done it a lot," he replied, giving a little shrug but not looking my way.

Water splattered us as we moved, hitting me in the face, and I closed my eyes, letting the sun warm my skin and thinking about my first few days here. How magical it had all seemed. I tried to grab hold of that feeling again, but it was impossible. The place was still gorgeous, the blue water still flawless as it shimmered under the sun and the islands breathtaking, but the appeal was gone. Dead just like my travel companions.

I opened my eyes when the boat began to slow.

We'd reached the area where the catamarans and monohulls were moored. There were half a dozen boats, spread out far enough apart that there was no danger of them banging into one another, and all of them were seemingly deserted.

The one we were headed toward had the number fifty-two on the side—which I now knew was its length in feet—and the word *Liberty* printed across the side in fancy script. Like Boone had said, it was smaller than the boat I'd spent the last two weeks on, but still a good size, and I studied it as we pulled to a stop at the back. The sliding glass doors leading into the salon had been left open, and the sight of it made my gut clench.

Boone cut the engine and the motor went silent as we drifted toward the yacht, bumping gently against the back when we reached it. He grabbed the ladder and held firm to keep the dingy steady, his gaze moving to me.

"You first."

I didn't move.

"Moira?"

My gaze snapped from the open doors to him. "They're still here."

He blinked, looking confused, and gave a slight shake of his head.

"The bodies," I continued. "They're still here, aren't they? I hadn't thought about it before, but of course they are. And you've been gone for days, meaning they've just been—" I couldn't finish.

Boone exhaled. "Yeah. They're here. I moved them all to one cabin, but you're right. They're going to be pretty ripe, too. We'll have to work together to bring them up."

He meant carry them. The bodies. The *dead* bodies.

What then?

I shuddered as my gaze moved to the water, knowing what we were going to have to do but hating the thought. Of course, we couldn't just leave them on the boat. It wasn't sanitary and if they hadn't already started to stink, they would soon. But dumping the bodies into the water? I looked toward the island we'd just left, scanning the beach. It wouldn't exactly be a burial at sea because we were surrounded by islands, and the bodies would most likely wash up on the beach we'd just left or even another one. I pictured the beautiful white sands dotted with rotting corpses and my stomach lurched. It was so grotesque, so wrong. But was there anything else we could do?

"Moira," Boone said, drawing my attention back to him. "We don't have any other choice."

"I know," I whispered.

His head bobbed, his hazel eyes intent on mine for a few seconds longer before he nodded to the boat. "Climb aboard and I'll hand you the bags. Then we can tie off."

I exhaled, mimicked his nod, and forced my legs to move.

The dingy shifted under me despite the tight grip Boone had on the ladder, but after two weeks, I was practiced enough at climbing in and out to make it with little effort.

Once I was on, I held my hand out. "I can tie us off."

Boone lifted his eyebrows in surprise, but I understood. The kind of knot you used to secure a rope to a cleat wasn't something just anyone knew, and had this virus left us alone, I never would have picked it up. I would have had my vacation and gone home without ever thinking about the figure eight loop Captain Dan made whenever he'd tied the dingy off, and I definitely never would have asked him to show me.

"I've learned a lot over the last two weeks," I told Boone.

He only stared at me for a few seconds longer before passing me the rope, and once I had it, I climbed the couple steps to the deck so I could twist it around the cleat. Around the bottom once, then twisting it over the top, ensuring the end was secured under the line. I pulled it tight, tugging on it once to make sure

I'd done a good job, then turned back to Boone. He was already unloading the bags.

I lugged two up the steps to what I now knew was called the cockpit—although I still couldn't figure out why the outdoor area designated for eating and lounging was called that. I set them on the table then headed back for more just as Boone climbed aboard. He grabbed the last couple before heading up the stairs after me.

This time, I didn't stop in the cockpit, but instead headed into the galley, doing my best not to focus on the faint scent of decay hanging in the air. The kitchen was smaller than the one on our yacht, but when I knelt and opened the cold storage area, I discovered there was still plenty of room. It was practically empty, and all I had to do to make space for the food we'd scavenged was push aside a couple bottles of wine.

Boone set two bags on the counter. "I'll get the others."

"Okay," I said as I began unloading the ones he'd set down.

He was still gone when I heard the thump.

I froze, looking around. Had it come from inside the boat, or had something bumped against us? Maybe a log or some other debris had hit the hull as the waves tried to carry it to shore, or it could have been some kind of sea life. Or, God forbid, a body. It was possible we weren't the only ones who'd realized the necessity of unloading the bodies before they started to rot.

I waited, listening— For what? Another thump, maybe? I wasn't sure, and after a few seconds and no other noises, I pushed the thought from my mind. Maybe it was better not knowing what the sound had been.

I went back to loading the fridge and Boone reappeared a second later. He'd just set the last two bags down when another bang sounded. This time, all I could think about was the body of some poor soul thudding against our boat, and it made me shudder.

"What was that?" Boone asked.

"It has to be something in the water." I didn't look at him, letting him fill in the blanks himself.

"It sounded like it was coming from inside."

At that, I froze again, recalling how the salon doors had been open and wondering if someone had come aboard while Boone was gone. Maybe searching for supplies? No. That didn't make sense. We were on a boat. If someone was here, there would be a dingy. Even if they swam here from one of the other boats, there would be flippers or another indication that a person had climbed aboard. There was nothing, though.

"It couldn't have," I said just as yet another thud sounded.

This one was followed by others, making it impossible to deny where the sounds were coming from.

I slowly stood, my gaze moving to the staircase to my right, which Boone was also looking at. Neither one of us said a word as the thuds continued, or even when they were joined by a scratching sound that reminded me of nails on a chalkboard. The hair on the back of my neck stood on end, but it wasn't from the bumps or scratches. It was from the barely audible moan.

"What the hell is that?" Boone's voice was low, but there no sign of the dread that had built inside me on his face. "That's where I put them." His gaze snapped to me. "You don't think they could still be alive, do you? I mean, I don't see how." He was shaking his head when he took a step forward. "They were dead. I checked their pulses."

He moved closer to the stairs, his confusion growing more intense by the second. I couldn't get my brain to work well enough to form any kind of theory about what the sound could be, but I knew one thing. There was no way Boone could have mistaken a live person for a dead one. I'd watched six people die the last few days, watched the color drain from their faces, watched the life go out of their eyes. There was no confusing that. The other thing I was certain of made even less sense than thinking Boone had made a mistake like that.

He needed a weapon.

I snapped out of my stupor when he took one more step toward the stairs.

"Stop." I rushed toward him, grabbing his arm to stop him from going any farther. "Don't go down there."

His gaze snapped to me. "But someone has to be alive. Why else would there be banging?"

"If they are alive, Boone, why wouldn't they just open the door?"

"They're delirious?" He didn't sound at all convinced. "I don't know. I just know someone is moving around in there."

"Or *something*."

I didn't even know what made me say the words, but once they were out, I knew I was right. As crazy as it seemed, it was the only thing that made sense. Even though it didn't really, because what I was thinking couldn't possibly be real.

I focused on the floor, not wanting to look him in the eye when I uttered the next word. "Zombies."

Boone let out a nervous laugh. "You can't be serious."

Forcing myself to look up, I held his gaze. "I know it sounds crazy but think about it. Is there another explanation? You watched them die, didn't you?"

His Adam's apple bobbed when he swallowed, and he nodded.

"Do you really think you made a mistake about that?"

Boone shook his head.

"Then you need to be prepared."

He blinked, his expression confused. Seemingly unable to form words or grasp what I was trying to say.

"A knife, Boone," I said, emphasizing the words. "Don't go in there without a way to protect yourself."

His gaze moved from me to the kitchen at my back as he gnawed on his bottom lip, and after only a second of thought, he pulled from my grasp and headed that way. My heart thudded as he dug through drawers. Trying to wrap my brain around this insane situation was impossible, because it just didn't make sense. It was crazy. It couldn't be real.

Deep down, I knew it was.

Boone came back with two of the biggest kitchen knives I'd ever seen, barely glancing my way when he held one out to me. "Here."

I took it, my hands trembling as I wondered if I'd even be able to use the thing. The thought of stabbing someone—even a dead someone—made my legs wobble and my stomach twist. What if it was the only way? What if sinking this knife into another person was the only thing that would save me?

I stared at the knife as Boone made his way down the stairs but snapped out of it when he stopped outside the bedroom door. The thudding had not only continued but seemed to have grown in intensity at the sound of the approaching footsteps. More moans had penetrated the thin door as well, but nothing about the noise was human. I couldn't help thinking about horror movies friends and I had watched as kids. Supernatural creatures that roamed the night and undead beings that dragged themselves across foggy fields, looking for something to sink their teeth into. Brains had always been what zombies craved in movies, but I couldn't imagine that *real* undead beings would care what they ate as long as it was fresh and bloody.

Boone glanced my way when a hysterical sounding laugh burst out of me, his hand reaching for the door. Realizing he needed backup, I hurried down a couple steps, stopping in the middle of the staircase since I didn't want to crowd him. There was so little space down here. So little room for error. What if all of them rushed from the room at once?

"How many people were on your boat?"

"Four others." He didn't look back at me. "A couple and their son, plus one more crew member."

My head bobbed as my hand tightened on the knife. "Okay."

He mimicked my gesture, then took a deep breath. "Are you ready?"

"Yeah." I had to force the word out because it was a lie.

Boone took another breath, held it, blew it out, then slowly turned the knob.

The door opened inward, which meant he had to shove it. It banged into whatever was trying to get out and a couple thuds followed. More moans sounded as a wave of warm, rotten air rushed into the hallway. I gagged but forced the contents of my stomach to stay down as Boone hurried forward and out of sight. He was swearing, and the sound of a scuffle had my heart jumping to my throat. I hurried down the last couple steps, and my eyes widened at the sight in front of me.

The things that used to be people were human no more. They had gray, rotting skin and milky eyes, and they were chomping at the air as Boone worked to hold them back. One was already down, this one smaller than the others, and Boone had kicked another one back—a woman—but she was already trying to get to her feet. His left hand was around the neck of one of the undead men when he stabbed the second in the eye, and dark blood that looked black in the shadowy room oozed out, making the already foul air twice as repulsive. I barely had time to focus on that before Boone had pulled his blade free, though. The thing—zombie—he'd killed dropped to the floor, and a second later, Boone stabbed the blade into the eye of the other one.

The woman managed to get to her feet at that moment, her sights set on me. She was shockingly thin and wearing only a swimsuit and coverup. The white fabric flapped behind her like a flag as she stumbled toward me, her hands reaching, her mouth open. The moan she let out sent a chill shooting through me and I raised my knife, knowing the impact would be quick and violent.

She slammed into me, and I felt my knife sink into her body, cutting through the rotten flesh before hitting bone. I had my eyes squeezed shut, but when she didn't stop moving, I was forced to open them. My knife was in her chest, which hadn't fazed her at all. She was still struggling as blood dripped from the wound, landing on my bare skin, and I was so focused on trying to hold her back that I couldn't pull my blade free. It was then that I realized I should have aimed for her brain. It had been years since I'd watched anything zombie related, and it had never been a form of fiction I enjoyed, so the thought had never occurred to me. It should have, though. It was a stupid mistake.

"Moira!" Boone shouted.

A second later, the woman was jerked off me, my knife still lodged in her chest. She was thrashing, still trying to get at me as I lay on the floor staring up at her, watching as Boone's fingers tightened on her neck. He slammed his knife into the side of her head, through her ear and into her brain, and she went still.

Boone tossed her behind him without bothering to pull his knife free, then knelt, his hazel eyes taking me in. "You're okay? You weren't bitten, were you?"

Bitten?

I was wearing nothing but my little red bikini, and it suddenly hit me just how vulnerable I'd been. In the movies, zombie bites turned you into a zombie. Why hadn't we thought of that before opening the door? Why hadn't we taken some kind of precaution? Again, it had been a stupid mistake.

Fear gripped me as I looked myself over. I was covered in blood from the zombie I'd stabbed, but it wasn't red. I'd thought the light had been playing tricks on my eyes when I first saw it, but I'd been wrong. It was black and thicker than usual, almost as if it had started to congeal, and it stank like rot. Meaning I smelled, too.

As repulsive as it was, it made looking for any injuries faster, and once I registered the lack of red blood smeared across my skin, I was able to relax. "I'm okay."

Boone let out a sigh of relief and stood, pulling me with him. He kept his hand on my elbow as he looked back toward the room.

"You were right. They're zombies."

This was one instance where being able to say *I told you so* wasn't fun.

Four

felt like I was moving on autopilot as Boone and I lugged the man's body up the stairs and through the galley, then outside. We'd already tossed the other man overboard, and Boone felt certain he'd be able to get the woman and boy by himself, but the men were heavier, and he'd needed my help. I'd given it without complaint, but I had a feeling once we were done and reality slammed into me, I might just lose my mind. I felt on the verge of it already.

The first body had already been carried farther out to sea by the time we reached the back of the boat, and a strange sort of relief washed over me when I realized it wasn't heading for the nearby beach. The Baths were too beautiful to be littered with bodies.

I grunted as I lifted the man's legs, preparing to toss him over while Boone counted. "One. Two. Three."

We pushed him over the edge and a splash sounded a split second later.

I closed my eyes.

"I'll get the others," Boone said. "You can get cleaned up."

My eyes were still closed when his footsteps moved away from me, heading back inside. I was sweating and shaking, and I smelled of rot, but I couldn't make myself move or even open my eyes right away. Clean up? I wasn't sure if the showers worked and the idea of jumping in the water right now—even to rinse the sticky, black blood from my body—was repulsive. The bodies were still too close.

I opened my eyes at the sound of footsteps. Boone was heading my way, the much smaller body of the boy in his arms but thankfully wrapped in a sheet. His hazel eyes held mine as he walked to the side of the boat, but he shifted his focus to the body when he stopped.

"He was a nice kid." Boone exhaled. "He asked a lot of questions about how to sail and seemed really excited about everything we did. It was fun having him around."

I swallowed, thinking of the people I'd watched die over the last few days, their bodies still on our boat and rotting— Or not. Maybe they, too, had turned into the undead.

"I'm sorry," I said, speaking to them as much as to Boone.

"Me too," he replied.

He tossed the kid's body into the water and turned away, heading back inside for the mother.

Only a couple minutes passed before he reappeared carrying the woman's body, which was wrapped in a sheet just like her son's had been. It was then that I realized Boone wasn't just doing it to cover the people. It was to rid the boat of the bedding as well. The bodies had been lying on the sheets for days, slowly rotting. They had to smell and were most likely soiled, making them useless to us. Probably, that entire room was useless. There was no way we'd be able to air out the stink any time soon.

I sank to the floor as Boone threw the last body in.

He frowned when he turned to face me. "Don't you want to shower?"

"I wasn't sure if it was working or if I'd have to use the ocean." My gaze moved behind me, but I quickly looked away from the sight of the bodies bobbing on the surface like buoys, the white sheets spread out around them.

"The showers work." He held his hand out. "You can probably go through Gloria's things, too. Find something else to wear."

I looked down, frowning at the black soaked into the fabric of my favorite red swimsuit. It was garbage now. There was no way I'd ever be able to put it on without picturing that dead woman's face. And now I was about to go through her clothes.

"Moira," Boone said, drawing my focus to him. "It's going to be okay. I promise."

"Okay," I mumbled.

He gave a firm nod. "We'll use the port side since the starboard side is pretty useless at this point."

With my brain as muddled as it was, it took me a second to remember which was which. "The left?"

"Yeah. I'll take the bow if you want the stern."

Those terms I knew. The bow was the front, the stern the back.

"Okay."

Boone gave me a small, exhausted looking smile. "Once we're cleaned up, we can sail to your boat and get your things."

My gut clenched at the thought, and I shook my head. "Forget it."

"What?" His smile melted away. "Don't you want to get your stuff?"

"I can't face that, Boone." Bile rose in my throat that I had to swallow down. "This was horrible enough, but if I have to see Sylvia or Bridge running at me, trying to take a bite out of me…" I shuddered and hugged myself. "Forget it. I can't do it."

Boone's frown deepened, but he nodded. "If you change your mind, let me know."

"I will," I said, although I knew my mind was made up. I also knew one other thing that I couldn't bring myself to voice. I could barely even acknowledge it to myself.

I wouldn't be going home. Probably ever.

I HAD MY WET HAIR WRAPPED IN A TOWEL AS I DUG through Gloria's closet. She'd clearly been a fan of Lilly

Pulitzer, and her closet was stuffed with the designer's clothes. Pastel pinks and greens and blues screamed at me as I searched for something to wear. Everything was so busy, and something about the brightly colored prints seemed almost irreverent considering our situation. Plus, it was all beach wear. Dresses made of thin, flowing fabric. Linen shorts. Tops with tiny spaghetti straps. Not exactly practical.

After deciding beggars couldn't be choosers—we were on a yacht, after all—I finally settled on a simple white sundress and pink two-piece swimsuit. Not putting one on would have been stupid since there was little chance of making it from the boat to land without getting a little wet. Even in the dingy.

After getting dressed and towel drying my hair, I headed back up.

Boone was at the helm, working coordinates into the navigation system, and he looked up when I stopped next to him, his gaze moving over me in an appraising way. "Feel better?"

"I feel cleaner," I said.

His head bobbed like he understood. "Yeah."

"Sorry my shower was so long. We were low on water, so it's been a few days since I took one and I felt gross after—"

I chose not to elaborate.

"No problem." He turned his gaze back to the computer. "I have the coordinates put in and I pulled the dingy up already."

I glanced back to find it hanging in its usual place at the back.

"Now we just have to untie the boat and get going." Boone's eyes were on me when I looked back. "Can you do that?"

"Untie the boat?"

"From the mooring ball," he elaborated.

"Yeah. I can do that." I straightened my back. "I've actually gotten pretty good at grabbing the mooring ball, too. When we get to the next place, I mean."

The first few times we'd moored the boat, I'd barely paid attention. I'd been too focused on my surroundings and too busy trying to relax, plus I'd known Captain Dan and John would take care of things. Once reality set in and I realized we were in danger, though, I'd started paying attention and even helping out, and had been surprised by how easy it all ended up being.

He smiled. "Good. That will be helpful."

I headed to the front of the boat while Boone started the engine. The mooring ball—a buoy that floated on the surface of the water and was permanently connected to a large, heavy anchor attached to the ocean floor—bobbed in the water, the ropes that kept us from floating away pulled tight. Before coming on this trip, I'd assumed we'd drop anchor everywhere we went, but I'd been wrong. Coral reefs were protected and dropping anchor was illegal in many places, making renting a mooring ball essential.

I knelt, ready to undo the ropes when the time came. Boone drove the boat forward to give the lines some slack and I undid the rope wrapped around the cleat on the port side, quickly pulling it through the loop at the top of the mooring ball and up out of the water. Once it was on the deck, I moved to the starboard side and repeated the process, being careful to make certain none of the rope was hanging over.

Then I stood and turned to face Boone, giving him a thumbs up.

He smiled.

I stayed at the bow long enough to make sure he didn't run over either the mooring ball we'd just detached from or any of the others bobbing in the water but headed back once we made it past without incident.

Boone smiled when I climbed up to stand at his side. "Good job."

"I can do the little stuff at least." I shrugged. "But

that's about it. Honestly, I don't know what I would have done if I hadn't run into you. I guess I would have stayed on the island and eventually started walking. Maybe I would have run into someone."

"Or you would have run into zombies." He shook his head like he still couldn't believe it. "You think it was a fluke?"

"The zombies?"

"Yeah. I mean, do you think everyone who dies from this virus eventually turns into one of them, or do you think it's only a few people here and there?"

I looked over my shoulder, back at the boats we'd passed then toward land. Part of me expected to see figures stumbling around, both on the beaches and the boats, but there was nothing. It did, however, remind me of the figure I'd seen in the distance, back when we were still at the restaurant. Had that been a zombie?

I wrapped my arms around myself and turned back to face the front. "I don't know what's happening, but I have a feeling we'll find out soon enough."

"Yeah," Boone said, his frown deepening.

We stood side by side in silence as we motored toward the other side of Virgin Gorda, the island stretching out beside us and seemingly empty. It didn't have a huge population, less than four thousand if I remembered correctly, but the first time we sailed past, we'd been able to see people driving on the few roads visible from the water and hanging out on the beaches. There had been other boats, too. Monohulls and catamarans, as well as a few mega yachts and even some smaller fishing and power boats. Now, though, there was nothing.

"Where are we going?" I asked when I found it impossible to stay silent any longer.

"Leverick Bay," Boone said. "It's at the north end of the island and has a little hotel as well as some restaurants and a marina. It's a good place to refuel and fill up on water if you need it." He glanced toward me. "If there are people, they might be congregating there. If not, we can at least go ashore and raid the bar and restaurants."

I could only nod, because at this point, I didn't have a lot of hope of finding people. I didn't know the statistics for this thing, but I did know it seemed pretty deadly. It was actually a miracle Boone and I hadn't gotten sick.

Without thinking, I put my hand on his. "I'm glad I'm with you."

His gaze darted to me, moving over my face and then down, and a flush spread across my cheeks as I thought about how we'd stood talking on the dock the morning we set off. How adorable he'd been, how he'd looked at me with quiet interest, making my blood sizzle. As odd as it sounded, I felt the same thing now. A heat between us that couldn't be denied. What was more, I could tell he felt it, too.

"Why are you here, Moira?" he asked.

My hand slipped from his and I looked away. Even after everything that had happened, I found it difficult to talk about the events that had brought me to this place. It was so stupid, especially because I now realized how lucky I'd gotten.

"I got dumped," I said, and more heat spread up my cheeks. That made it sound so silly. So petty. "Not just dumped." I forced myself to meet Boone's gaze and to my relief, saw no judgement there. "I was engaged. His name was Michael. We'd been together for years. Seven to be exact."

"Seven years?" he said, shock ringing in his words.

"We met in college and started dating. Kept dating after we graduated, then moved in together. We'd been engaged for three years and were three months from the wedding."

"That's when he dumped you?"

"That was when we won the lottery."

Boone blinked, and the shock on his face forced a laugh out of me. People never saw that part of the story coming.

"The lottery?" he said.

"Two hundred million dollars to be exact," I said. "I don't usually tell people how much I won, but let's face it, it doesn't make much of a difference now."

Boone's mouth dropped open.

My smile widened, and a sudden thrill shot through me at the idea of getting this off my chest. I wanted to spill the beans about my sad, failed relationship. Wanted to lay out the whole ugly truth and be done with it.

"We bought the ticket together and were shocked when we won," I continued. "All I could think about were the places we could go. How we could buy a house right away. How we would never have to worry about money. We would be able to give our kids everything they would ever need and even things they didn't need. It had felt like my happily-ever-after. I thought Michael was thinking the same thing. I'd been wrong."

"Don't tell me he cheated on you or something," Boone said, his disgust at the idea apparent.

"What he did was worse," I said. "Michael turned the ticket in, claiming the money for himself. He didn't come home after that, and he stopped answering my calls. He unfriended me on social media and started telling people we'd broken up. I didn't know what was going on, and at first, I didn't even realize he had the ticket. Honestly, at that point, I was more confused about why things had fallen apart than concerned about the money. It wasn't until a mutual friend told me he'd won the lottery that I'd even remembered the ticket. I was furious, but so hurt, too. I didn't even care about the money anymore, but my family convinced me to hire a lawyer, so I sued him."

"Did you win?" Boone looked like he was on the edge of his seat.

"I did." I shrugged to illustrate just how little I cared. Then or now. "It was easy once we got security footage from the store, not only proving we'd bought the ticket together, but that it had been *my* money. The judge awarded me half, plus damages for trying to steal it, plus he forced Michael to pay my parents back for the wedding. After it was all said and done, he walked away with about ten million dollars. Still a lot, but nothing compared to what he would have had if he'd stayed with me."

"Why?" Boone asked, voicing the question that had been nagging at me for the past two years. The one that still haunted me. "Why did he do it?"

"He'd said he felt trapped. That after seven years, he felt like he couldn't leave me even though he wasn't happy. He said he saw the ticket as a sign that he was supposed to leave."

Boone snorted. "So, he thought he'd just steal it?"

"That was what the judge said." I let out a long sigh, feeling as if a weight had just been lifted off my shoulders. "I spent the next two years sulking, barely spending the money. I didn't buy new furniture or clothes. Didn't even quit my job as a first-grade teacher. It was like I was stuck."

"Why this trip?" Boone waved to the boat. "What changed?"

"My family wouldn't stop bugging me to move on," I explained. "Then one day a coworker came in talking the sailing trip her parents had taken. She showed me the pictures, and something just clicked. I booked the trip that day. I thought it would get my family off my back, but also that it might help me snap out of it."

"That's—" Boone paused as if trying to figure out what to say, then snorted out a laugh. "Incredible."

"It's stupid, honestly. I mean, I was mourning the death of this relationship for two years, wasting my time wishing Michael had stuck around. How stupid is that? He saved me from making a huge mistake! I should have been thanking him. That's the incredible part."

"That," Boone said, his gaze holding mine, "and the fact that you dated someone so stupid. I mean, what kind of moron would leave you?"

A flush spread across my cheeks and I looked away. That heat was back, simmering between us the way it had on the dock. Like a fire was building.

Boone cleared his throat, breaking the spell.

His focus was once again on the ocean in front of us when I looked at him. We were rounding the end of the island, and soon a marina came into view, as well as a tiki bar and a hotel. There was a small pool too, and beyond that, a hotel and restaurant.

No one was in sight.

A few boats were moored nearby, but they looked as empty as the island did.

"Looks pretty deserted," I said.

"Yeah." Boone sighed. "We'll grab a mooring ball and get the dingy down. If anyone is around, the sound of our motor should draw them out."

"And we should probably take the knives."

"Yeah." Boone's brows furrowed. "I just wish we had something a little better."

"At least they're sharp," I muttered even though I agreed with him.

Boathook in hand, I climbed from the helm and headed for the bow while Boone slowed the boat. Directing him which way to go and how fast while I also leaned down to grab the mooring ball was the tricky part. I was tall, thankfully, but it was still a stretch, and I didn't always get it on my first try, forcing the captain to go around and approach again.

Holding the hook out in front of me so I could point to the ball bobbing on the water, I looked back toward Boone, who had an expression of concentration on his face. Once we were close enough, I knelt and extended the hook to give myself a better reach.

"Almost!" I called loud enough that Boone would hear me.

The boat drifted closer, and I leaned down,

skimming the hook across the surface of the water in hopes of catching the rope attached to the mooring ball. I managed to grab it on the first try, then quickly pulled it up and grabbed the rope on the port side, so I could thread it through the loop and wrap the end around the cleat. Then I repeated the process with the rope attached to the starboard side. When I was done, I stood and turned to face Boone, who was smiling.

"Good job."

"The hardest part is getting the rope out of the water." I headed his way, boathook still in hand. "I miss sometimes, but for the most part, I'm getting the hang of it."

"You did good," he said, cutting the engine. "Really."

I beamed under his praise.

We worked together to lower the dingy, then loaded the few bags we had. We didn't need to worry about snorkel gear since we could drive right up to the dock, but we did make sure to bring the knives. Which I laid carefully in the bottom of the boat, not wanting to puncture it.

I perched on the side of the dingy while Boone worked to get the motor going. My gaze was bouncing from boat to boat, hoping someone would appear, but they looked as empty and abandoned as they had when we first pulled up.

Boone expertly maneuvered the dingy between the other boats as he headed toward the dock, while I held onto the rope, ready to tie us up.

The first day after John got sick, I'd felt totally useless, but Captain Dan had worked hard to show me things. Now, I wondered if he'd been worried about me being left alone and wanted to ensure I knew how to take care of myself at least a little. I wasn't positive, but either way, I was thankful to him for taking the time to teach me.

The tide was low, meaning the dock felt like it was towering over me when we reached it, but I managed to tie the dinghy to the cleat. Once that was done, Boone climbed up and I passed him the bags—and set the knives on the dock—then he reached down and grabbed me under the armpits, hauling me up.

He scooped the knives up and held one out to me, saying, "Be ready. Stay alert."

I nodded, my heart thumping erratically as I remembered the way the zombies had charged us in the boat. We had more space here, meaning more chance for escape, but more potential to be overrun by a bigger group as well.

Knife in hand, Boone headed down the dock and I followed. The hand clutching my own knife was shaky, and I clung to it as hard as I could.

A few chickens pecked at the beach, and I contemplated the possibility of catching a few. Even if we managed, would we know what to do with them? We could keep them and hope they laid eggs, or we could wring their necks and pluck the feathers. Then what? How did you prepare a chicken that hadn't already been cleaned out? I didn't have a clue.

It seemed more likely that we'd be able to catch some fish. Boone practically lived on a boat. He had to know how to clean a fish.

"We should get some fishing poles." I kept my voice low, but amidst the silence, it still made me jump.

Boone looked over his shoulder. "That's actually a great idea."

Like the little restaurant at The Baths, this place had a small pool for tourists to use. Signs telling people where they could rent gear for various water sports were tacked to the wall, as well as one for the restaurant and another that told people where they could find the restrooms. There was also a big sign advertising Pusser's Rum, and I found myself thinking about earlier today when Boone and I drank together. It felt like more than just a few hours had passed, but that was all it had been.

Boone headed for the restaurant, and I followed,

my gaze darting around. I expected something to run out at us at any second, but the only things moving were the chickens. That was when it occurred to me that most people had probably died locked inside buildings.

"They won't be able to get out," I said, then shook my head when Boone shot me a questioning look. "The dead, I mean. People were inside when they died. In their houses or hotel rooms. On their boats. Zombies can't open doors."

"That should help." His eyes darted around as if he, too, expected something to come charging toward us. "Although, I wouldn't take for granted that we're safe. One could still sneak up on us."

"You don't have to worry about that," I told him.

The restaurant was dark, but luckily, Boone had thought ahead. I stood at his side, tense and on edge as he pulled a flashlight from his bag and flicked it on, panning it around to illuminate the corners of the room. The tables were set as if waiting for someone to arrive for dinner, flatware and cloth napkins sitting beside plates where they would remain indefinitely.

I followed Boone when he started walking, the two of us silent as we moved through the room, then into the kitchen. It was as dark and empty as the dining area, but it, too felt like it was waiting for people to arrive. No one would, though, and I thought about time stretching out. About dust settling on everything. About a hurricane sweeping through and breaking windows or damaging the roofs, and how slowly time and nature would work together to reclaim this island. It was a sad thought.

Boone inhaled when he reached the fridge, almost like he was holding his breath as he waited to find out if the contents were salvageable. Since the power on the other side of the island only went off this morning, odds were good we'd be okay, but that didn't stop me from whispering a silent prayer.

Cool air rushed out when he opened it, and a

smile stretched across his face.

"Let's load up as much as we can." He glanced back at me. "We can make a couple trips if we have to."

"This won't all fit in our cold storage," I reminded him, thinking about the small fridge on our boat.

"There's another below deck," he said, not looking back at me.

"That's a relief," I muttered, mostly to myself.

Boone grabbed a few items and shoved them in his bag, and I did the same. Fruit and vegetables, eggs and meat. We filled all six of our bags in a matter of minutes, but even then, there was so much left. Making a second trip would definitely be necessary.

"The sun's going to be setting soon," Boone said as we headed out, each of us loaded down with food. "We should moor here for the night and come back to shore in the morning. Load up again and then decide what to do."

"Are we going to head to Tortola?" I asked, barely noticing the empty tables as I followed him through the restaurant because I was too busy thinking about the long, exhausting trip here.

After landing in St. Thomas—which was in the US Virgin Islands—I'd taken a cab to the dock then a one-hour ferry ride to Tortola where I'd had to take another cab so I could catch a second ferry to Scrub Island. Tortola was the biggest and most populated island in the British Virgin Islands, and if we were going to find some form of civilization, it would probably be there.

"I guess that's our best bet." Boone was frowning when he glanced at me. "I know you're hoping to make it back to the US, but I have to be honest, I don't know if that's plausible. If this virus has decimated everything else the way it has Virgin Gorda, it's not going to be easy."

"I know," I said, sighing, shaking my head.

That was when it occurred to me that I knew

nothing about him. He was American, that much I was sure of, but he only talked about *me* getting back to the states. Was the US not his home anymore?

"What about you?" We were almost to the door when I adjusted the heavy bags I was carrying, shifting the weight so the straps didn't dig into my skin so much. "Don't you want to make it back to the states?"

"I'm fine." His shoulders rose and fell as he pushed the restaurant's front door open, holding it for me as I stepped out into the hot Caribbean day. "I don't really have any family to speak of. A couple distant cousins, but that's about it. I've lived here for years."

"Why here?" I was half focused on what we were talking about and half on our surroundings, and I paused to look around, squinting from the bright sun.

"I grew up sailing," he explained. "We lived in Miami and my parents had a boat. It was what we always did. We came here on vacation when I was sixteen and loved it. Best place I've ever been. My parents died the next year in a car accident and I went to live with my grandma, but she died a few weeks after I graduated from high school. I didn't know what else to do with myself, so I moved here. I've been sailing for different charter companies ever since."

"Wow."

It was impressive, thinking about him throwing caution to the wind and moving so far away from everything he knew when he was so young. Being his own person. It also made the past two years I'd spent sulking over my failed relationship seemed doubly pathetic. How could some people be so strong in the face of adversity while others floundered and even drowned? For two years I'd done nothing, but he'd immediately moved on despite great loss and had been here ever since.

I looked him up and down, wondering exactly how long he'd been here. "You're what? Thirty?"

Boone gave me a lopsided grin. "Thirty-one. You?"

"Twenty-nine."

We stared at each other as we headed for the dock, heat simmering between us, and the quiet wrapped around us. Boone's gaze traveled to my lips, and I sucked in a breath, nearly gagging when the putrid stink of rot filled my nostrils.

My eyes widened and I tore my gaze from his, looking around just as the dead woman lunged at me. Her mouth was open, her hands grabbing, but I managed to stumble out of reach. She fell, but scrambled toward me on her hands and knees, trying to get up but unable to, and the movement was so sickeningly unnatural that it made me tremble. I dropped my bag and let out a scream, swinging my knife at the thing. Boone, too, had dropped his things, and like me, he had his knife out, but he was steadier and more prepared and managed to get hold of the woman's shirt. Too bad it was a thin, gauzy swimsuit cover and ripped in seconds.

Boone cursed and tossed the fabric aside as the woman continued moving toward me. She was in only a small bikini now, the black fabric barely covering her decaying body. The sight was the most repulsive thing I'd ever seen. The way her gray, saggy breasts bounced as she moved toward me. How the bottom had ridden up, revealing one gray butt cheek.

Boone grabbed her before she could make it to me, his grip on her hair this time so she couldn't pull free. She was still thrashing when he slammed the blade of his knife into the base of her neck and up into her brain. She stopped moving so quickly it looked like someone had pulled the plug on her, then fell to the ground with a thud when he dropped her. Then he was hurrying toward me, reaching out, patting my arm. Trying to make sure I was all right.

"Are you okay? Please, tell me you're okay."

"I'm okay."

"Shit, Moira," he was panting, out of breath from the confrontation and worry. "I'm sorry. I got too comfortable."

His gaze moved over me one more time as if trying to make sure I was okay but paused on my breasts. That was when I realized that not only had the shoulder of my dress slipped down, but that my suit had also shifted during the struggle and my left breast was out.

I yanked the dress up, flushing, and Boone released me.

He sat back, swallowing, then let out a long breath. "We should go back to the boat. It's safer there."

"Yeah," I said, my voice low, my hand still holding the dress in place while my cheeks burned.

I got to my feet, pausing to arrange my swimsuit before grabbing my bags. Boone and I headed to the dock in silence, the mood tense but charged as well. When we reached the dingy, I climbed in first and he handed me the supplies we'd managed to pilfer, then he was climbing in, too. He got the motor ready while I undid the rope, making sure it was completely out of the water. We still hadn't said a word when he started the engine.

I looked back at the shore as he drove toward the boat. A figure emerged from between a couple buildings and stumbled toward the sound of our motor. The chickens distracted it, though, and I watched as it lumbered after them, its movements much too slow and uncoordinated to catch the animals. The sight would have been funny if I'd seen it in a movie. A zombie stumbling in circles, trying to catch a chicken. In reality, though, it wasn't the least bit amusing.

<h1 style="text-align:right">Five</h1>

e worked as a team when we reached the boat, still not talking. Boone held the dingy steady while I climbed aboard and secured the rope to the cleat, then he passed me the bags. Once he was on, I headed into the galley, my arms loaded down with supplies. My heart was still pounding from the close call, but that wasn't the only reason my pulse was faster than usual, and I knew it. I was thinking about being on this boat all night with Boone. About the unmistakable attraction between us. About what might happen.

It was stupid and irresponsible. We shouldn't be focused on each other in the middle of all this. Then again, there was a part of me that thought it was the best idea I'd ever had. What was a better distraction from the undead walking the Earth than a hot guy? And wasn't it okay to need a distraction considering everything going on? I was only human, after all,

Boone came into the galley behind me as I unloaded the bags, and I stiffened when I felt his hands on my shoulders. "Moira."

I turned to face him, his hands staying on my skin, caressing me as I spun. He was staring at me, his gaze intent. The fire in them unmistakable.

"I'm sorry."

"It's not your fault," I assured him. "We were both distracted."

"I'm still sorry."

"Me, too."

Boone swallowed, seemed unsure of what to say, then just stared at me.

I thought about what could happen next. It had been two years since I'd had sex. Not since Michael. How sad was that? Even worse, how sad would it be if I died without ever having sex again? Not just sad. Pathetic.

My gaze moved to Boone's lips, and he sucked in a breath.

I whispered his name and took a step closer to him, and he nodded as if giving me permission.

I pressed my lips to his, and in seconds, every ounce of hesitation was gone. Boone's arms went around me, and he pulled me close, the kiss deepening until I could feel it in my toes. His tongue brushed my lips and I opened to him, allowing him to explore my mouth while his hands moved down my back. He squeezed my ass, pulling me closer, and I moaned when I felt him press against my stomach. Then he was reaching lower, grabbing the hem of my sundress and pulling it up. We broke the kiss long enough for him to yank it over my head, but we were back on each other before he'd even had a chance to toss it aside. Once he had, his hands moved up, cupping my breasts, his thumbs teasing my nipples through the thin fabric of my swimsuit. I gasped, and he teased me more, twisting them lightly and sending a jolt of pleasure through my body.

We continued to kiss as we stumbled outside, making it to the lounge area and toppling down. I was on top of him, straddling him. My hips moving in circles, his moving up to meet mine. Even with the barrier of our swimsuits separating us, the feel of him against me was magical. How had I gone this long without having a man inside me? Why had I wanted to?

Boone worked to undo my swimsuit top as we kissed, my body gyrating against his. It fell free and his hands covered my breasts, his skin warm against mine, the callouses on his palms from his years of sailing driving my sensitive nipples wild. He pulled me closer, and his mouth closed over my right nipple, making me gasp. He sucked and teased, drawing sounds out of me I'd never made before. Then he moved to my left nipple, giving it the same treatment. He took turns after that, teasing one and then the other, sucking on them, nipping at them gently with his teeth. The feeling was heavenly, and it helped push every other thought and worry from my mind. Helped me forget all the horror I'd seen over the last few days. Helped me forget that I might have lost everything. It was just Boone and me, and that was all I needed.

Without warning, he rolled me onto my back, settling at my side so he could run his hand down my body as we kissed. His fingers grazed my breasts but didn't stop, instead continuing down where they paused to trace an intimate line across my stomach before finally slipping into my swimsuit. The feel of his fingers brushing my sensitive flesh made me moan, and I opened my legs, giving him better access. He took full advantage of it, teasing me until I was writhing, then finally plunging inside. I gasped and squeezed my eyes shut, savoring the feeling. I was so hot, and so close.

His mouth returned to my breasts, and I relished the dual sensations while my body hummed and the need inside me built. It was like a fire, growing hotter and hotter by the second until finally there was an explosion. I cried out, my back arching off the cushion, my toes curling, my body throbbing with ecstasy as wave after wave crashed into me.

It took a couple seconds to come down, but once I had, I lifted my gaze to Boone's. He was staring at me like he was considering devouring me, his focus solely on my face as I moved my hand to his chest, sliding it down, stopping when I reached the waistband of his swim trunks. I pulled them down, allowing him to spring free, and wrapped my hand around him. It was my turn to tease him, and his moans told me I was doing a good job as I moved my hand up and down, slow at first, then faster. Then slow again. He was grunting, his face twisted in an expression I found so sexy I could barely catch my breath as I continued to work him over. Deep down, I knew how crazy and wrong all this was, but I couldn't care. Not with my body still humming and not with this amazingly sexy, half-naked man at my side.

"Stop," he said out of nowhere, covering my hand with his. "I want to be inside you."

I swallowed and released him, unable to talk. Boone shifted so he was on his knees, pulling his swim trunks off the rest of the way and tossing them aside. He hovered over me, his gaze taking me in before settling on my own swimsuit bottoms. I shifted, allowing him to pull them down, over my ass to my thighs, his eyes following their trail. Once they were gone, his gaze moved back up, and I shivered at the expression in his eyes. It was carnal and possessive, and unlike anything I'd ever seen in Michael's eyes. All those years together, and he'd never looked at me like this. Never looked at me like I was the only thing he needed to be happy.

Boone moved up my body, kissing me as he went. Then he nudged my legs apart and settled between them, his gaze holding mine for just a second before he pushed his way inside.

It felt so good. Slow and steady, him stretching me. Filling me. Making me moan. He paused when he was all the way in, but only for a moment. Then he started moving, slow at first, then faster. I gripped his shoulders, holding on. Digging my nails in. Biting down on my lower lip to keep from moaning. No one was around to hear us, but I still held it in. I didn't even know why.

"God," he said against my ear as he thrust into me. "You feel so good."

"So do you," I gasped, barely able to find my voice.

Boone shifted so he was grabbing my hips, then he really started moving. It was hard and fast, and every thrust made my body hum, and every inch of him made me pulse with need. I hadn't known how much I'd missed sex until this moment, but with him inside me, with his hot skin against mine, I suddenly felt like this trip was the best decision I'd ever made.

He came just as I did a second time, thrusting hard and grunting out his release, then staying there for a moment. Him on top of me, his skin sweaty against mine. When he'd caught his breath, he rolled off me and we lay side by side, gasping.

We stayed that way long after we'd both stopped panting, watching as the sun set over the Caribbean. We were naked, but neither of us minded. There was no one around to see us, after all. No one alive, anyway.

"I guess if you have to be stranded somewhere," I said, my focus on the bright pinks and oranges spreading across the sky, "there are worse places to be."

"And worse people to be with," he said, running his hand down the side of my face.

I shifted my gaze so I could look at him, and decided the sunset was nothing compared to the man in front of me. I barely knew him, and while this thing between us was mostly lust at this point, that didn't mean I wasn't lucky to have found him. He was capable and smart, self-sufficient, and he'd put confidence in me when a lot of other people might have questioned if I could do it. For that, I was thankful.

MY FIRST FEW NIGHTS ON A BOAT, IT HAD COME AS A shock just how well I'd slept. My room had been small but the bed nice, and the constant rocking was gentle enough to be soothing rather than jarring. That was when the air conditioning had been on every night, though. Once we'd had to stop using it—to save power and because almost everyone had been burning with fever and freezing—it had gotten a little more difficult. There were windows in the cabin, little portholes that opened just enough to let air in but didn't necessarily work great when it came to air flow. It had caused more than a couple sweaty nights, but typically, I'd been so exhausted at the end of the day that I'd had no trouble falling asleep.

That was also the case with Boone at my side. His catamaran either had better air flow or I was less worried about the heat, because I didn't wake up drenched in sweat even once. In fact, I didn't wake up at all until the sun had begun to rise, at which point I stirred, slowly emerging from a dreamless sleep and totally unsure of where I was.

I opened my eyes to a room I didn't recognize, instantly aware of the warm body at my side, and shifted. The sight of Boone's bare chest, rising and falling slowly, brought the day before back in a rush of conflicting emotions, and I closed my eyes once again.

Yesterday while we were having sex, and even a little after as we held each other, I'd been able to push away every thought that wasn't about Boone. But I'd known it was temporary, and in the light of day, all I could think about was my family back in Ohio. Some of them were gone, I knew, because no one who got this virus recovered. But not all of them had been sick the last time I was able to get through. Were any of them immune the way I was? Was this zombie thing going on there as well? I couldn't imagine it had skipped the rest of the world only to doom those of us in the Caribbean, but anything was possible. Wasn't the existence of the dead proof of that?

The bed groaned as Boone shifted, and I opened my eyes to find him awake and staring at me, a somber expression on his face that matched the feelings surging through me.

"You okay?"

I shook my head. "No. Last night was a good distraction, but in the light of day, I can't ignore what's going on."

"I know." He ran the back of his hand down the side of my face. "I'm sorry."

"I haven't been able to get through to my family in more than a week, and my phone is dead now." I frowned, a thought suddenly occurring to me. "Does your cell phone work?"

"It's charged," he said, but his frown had deepened. "It isn't working, though, and even if it was, I don't have an international plan. No one in the states to call. Remember?"

"Oh yeah," I said with a sigh.

Boone brushed my dark hair out of my face, his gaze staying on me. "Tell me about them."

"My family?"

"Yeah."

I swallowed, a lump of tears rising in my throat. "We're a typical family, I guess. My parents are still married—been together for almost forty years. Both my older brother and younger sister are married with children, and I have two nieces and three nephews. We get together for holidays and other events, and generally get along, but they've been driving me nuts the last two years and I was looking forward to getting away." Again, I swallowed when tears threatened. "Now I feel like an ass. Especially when I think about never seeing them again."

"You don't know what's going to happen," Boone said.

"I know," I replied, but the words were soft. Just a whisper.

No, I didn't know what was going to happen. That was true. But there was one thing I did know for certain. Nothing was ever going to be the same. Even if I somehow made it home and found a few of them still alive, life as we knew it was done.

Boone and I stared at one another for a few seconds in silence, each of us lost in our thoughts, before he groaned and pushed himself up. "We should head back to shore and see what else we can find."

He was right. My vacation had ended the day the first person on our boat got sick, and there was no going back. Especially now. Now it would be hard work all day, because if we didn't work, we'd die. Either from lack of food and water or from something else. Zombies or maybe even storms.

Boone was already getting dressed when I dragged myself from bed. The swimsuit I pulled on felt entirely too skimpy after my close call with the zombie yesterday, but it was all I had. I topped it off with the same dress I'd worn the day before, then grabbed a pair of flip flops. Then together, Boone and I headed up. As my shoes flopped against the floor with each step I took, I couldn't help thinking about how awful it would be to have to run for my life in them. I needed to find something better.

"You know," I said as Boone and I worked to empty the remaining food from the bags, "We should think about finding some sturdier clothes. I mean, we don't know much about how this whole zombie thing works at this point, but we know how it worked in the movies. You get bitten and you turn. It could be different in real life, but I'm not sure if I'm willing to take a chance on that."

He paused in the middle of stuffing a few now empty bags into the one he planned to carry. "You're right. Although, this is Virgin Gorda, not Ohio. It's not like there's an abundance of pants and long-sleeved shirts. It's warm here all year round."

"True," I said with a sigh. "But some better shoes would be nice if nothing else."

Boone looked down at my feet, frowning at the flip flops before turning his gaze on his own feet. He wore boat shoes that were at least better for running than what I had on, but only a little.

"We'll see what we can find," he said before grabbing the supplies off the counter and heading for the door.

In no time we were loaded into the dinghy and headed for shore, the hum of the engine the only real noise in the otherwise quiet morning. The zombie we'd seen the night before was nowhere in sight, but since the chickens were still around, I wasn't sure where it had gone. Maybe it had been lured away by other, easier to catch prey.

If whatever distracted it had been human, I hoped they were able to get away.

I kept my eyes open as we approached the dock, wanting to make sure we were prepared if the noise we were making drew attention our way. Like the night before, there was no movement though. I must have been right in thinking that the majority of people died inside and couldn't get out, because even though the population of this island wasn't huge, it was big enough that we should have seen more than one or two of the dead at this point.

Assuming everyone came back. We didn't know for sure how it worked.

We repeated the process from yesterday, docking and tying off the dingy, then heading for the restaurant so we could pilfer more goods. We'd gotten everything we could from the refrigerator the night before, but there was more in the freezer that hadn't yet thawed, so we loaded that, then took as much of the nonperishable food as we could.

"We can probably make one more trip," Boone said as we slipped out of the restaurant. This time paying attention.

"Then what?"

He sighed, his gaze darting around as he pressed his lips together in thought, then said, "We can sail to a couple nearby islands and see if anyone is around. If so, we've found survivors. If not, we can load up on supplies. Both Necker Island isn't far."

"I haven't heard of that," I said risking a glance his way before once again focusing on our surroundings.

"It's owned by Richard Branson and has a private luxury resort. Honestly, it might be a good area to settle in."

My steps faltered but I didn't glance his way for

long, too busy keeping an eye out. "Settle?"

Boone slowed as well. "If we want to be safe from the dead, I mean." He sighed, acting like he didn't savor having to saying the next words. "I have to be honest, Moira. I do. We need to focus on is finding a safe place to stay until we can figure out what the long-term solution is. Sailing to the States right now is out of the question. I'm sorry. Maybe later, things will be different. Maybe help will come or— I don't know. I just know we need to focus on today before we can think about tomorrow."

He was right, but since I wasn't ready to totally accept that, I started walking faster and said, "And you think Necker Island will be a good place?"

"It will have rooms and restaurants and bars," he said, keeping stride with me, "and no one lives on them full time. Even if some of the staff or guests got sick and died there, the number of zombies would be minimal."

"Meaning they would be easier to kill off."

"Exactly," Boone replied.

The thud of our footsteps when we reached the dock marked the end of our conversation since the sound seemed entirely too loud in the silent day. A few nearby chickens squawked and ran off, and somewhere in the distance, a dog barked, but no zombies came running.

We made it back to the boat and unloaded before returning to shore so we could fill up for a third time, but still hadn't seen any sign of the dead by the time we were loading the dingy for the final time. It made me hope that the few creatures we'd seen were some kind of fluke and not everyone had turned from the virus. If that were the case, making it back to the states just might be possible. Somehow.

Back on the boat, we unloaded and got ready to set off, Boone at the helm while I moved to the bow, so I could undo the ropes from the mooring ball, and in no time, we were motoring out of the bay.

I was standing at his side as he drove past a catamaran a little smaller than ours when movement caught my eye. A second later, a figure emerged from the boat's salon, stumbling toward us with its arms raised. The sunken eyes and gray skin of what had once been a man told me he had been dead for a while, and the sight was doubly repulsive thanks to the various rips in the creature's skin. Black blood oozed from each puncture sight, as well as the thing's eyes, nose, ears, and mouth. The wind carried the sound of its moans to us, as well as the stink of death, and my stomach twisted. Bile filled my mouth, and even though it repulsed me, I swallowed it down, not wanting to waste the food and water I'd consumed. It wasn't easy holding back.

"God." Boone waved his hand in front of his face, then revved the motor.

"I guess it's something we're going to have to get used to," I said, watching the zombie as we passed the boat. "I mean, even if the dead don't come back, we're still going to have to deal with a lot of rotting bodies."

"Yeah," he said, letting out a long, exhausted breath.

The boat was behind us in no time, but the zombie didn't stop its pursuit. It continued along the deck, stumbling over ropes and pulleys, and bouncing off the lifelines. I thought it would stop once it reached the bow, but it didn't, and I watched in fascinated horror as its legs slammed into the wires that served as lifelines and the creature toppled forward, plummeting head over heels into the water below. It went under with a splash, resurfacing a second later with its limbs flailing. I continued watching, curious if it would be able to swim, but it was back under in a second. A few more times the thing's head emerged before the zombie finally sank and disappeared from sight.

I turned my back on it. "They can't swim."

"Good," Boone said. "If we can find an isolated island to hole up on, we might be okay."

"For how long?" I asked, squinting so I could peer up at him. "How long does this go on?"

"I don't know," he replied. "Until things return to normal? Until someone comes to find survivors? There has to be a refugee center or something, right?"

"Yeah," I mumbled.

I thought of disaster movies I'd watched over the years. How people who were trying to escape storms or wars or plagues would gather in one central location and wait for the government to help them. The thing about that, however, was that there needed to be a someone in charge who could organize help. What happened if no one was around to do that? What became of the people?

My mind went to other movies. *Mad Max* and even *Zombieworld*, that crazy comedy starring Hadley Lucas. In those movies, people had to figure out how to survive on their own, and in many cases, it wasn't hunger or thirst or even the dead that became their biggest worry. It was other survivors.

Once again, I wished we had something better than a couple kitchen knives to defend ourselves with.

Six

To help conserve the gas we had, Boone suggested we put the sails up shortly after leaving Leverick Bay. Like with everything else, it was something I never would have been able to do on my own, but I was more than capable of assisting him in. A boat of this size had two—the mainsail and the jib—but since we wanted to keep our pace leisurely, we elected to put up only the main, and in no time, the wind had caught it and was carrying us to our destination.

Like the day before when we left the Baths, the Island of Virgin Gorda seemed deserted. The distant sounds of cars or boats were no more, and there was no music or voices floating through the air. It was as if the entire population had disappeared, and Boone and I were the only ones left.

We stopped at a few ports and went ashore so we could gather anything that might be useful. Boone found fishing gear and more flippers and snorkels just in case. He found gas cans and filled them whenever he could, and I gathered as much water and packaged food as I could find. While having all those things was satisfying, I couldn't stop the terror from sweeping over me as hour after hour went by and still, we found no other survivors.

Necker Island was to be our final destination for the day, which Boone described as over seventy acres of luxury private island that catered to the rich. Despite the detailed description he'd given me, I was unprepared for the sight as we approached. The expansive white sand beaches overlooking crystal blue water, the villas that were nicer than anything I had ever set foot in. The bars. The restaurant. The tennis courts. It was a sight to behold.

"No mooring needed here," Boone said as he slowed the boat, preparing to pull up to the private dock.

"Of course not," I mumbled, unable to process the sight in front of me as I worked to take it all in.

"You ready?" Boone asked, an edge to his voice that jolted me out of my trance.

I scrambled across the boat and headed for the stern. This was something I'd never done – docking a boat – but I told myself it couldn't be that hard.

We'd already tied the bumpers to the side of the boat, which cushioned the impact when we bounced against the dock. My arms were shaking as I reached for the cleat, managing to grab hold on my first try. I twisted the rope around it while Boone held the boat steady, his teeth gritted as if to emphasize the work it was taking. My nerves were already frayed though, and my legs were trembling when I scrambled from the boat.

I secured the bow of the boat next, pulling the rope tight so there was very little space between it and the dock. Pulling such a big boat where you wanted it to go was surprisingly easy, but I guessed it shouldn't have been. Between the rope wrapped around the cleat and the water, the boat was pretty pliable in this position.

I stood when Boone came over to join me. He wasn't looking at me but was instead surveying the island, and I followed his gaze, searching for any movement that might indicate someone—or something—was around. There was nothing but the sway of the palm trees in the evening breeze and the lapping of the water against the beach.

"Looks pretty deserted," he said after a moment of contemplative silence.

"Yeah," I mumbled, my gaze moving around the area. "No other boats."

He let out a long, tired sounding breath, then

turned his focus to me. "Stay close and alert. Even after we look around. The island isn't huge, but it is more than seventy acres, which is a lot of ground to cover. We don't want one of those things catching us off guard again."

I shuddered, remembering the milky eyes and rotten flesh of the undead woman who'd tried to take a bite out of me. It had been a close call and I had no desire to revisit it, which meant keeping my eyes open.

A small structure with some watersport equipment was visible to our right, which was the direction Boone headed. Like every other place we'd come to, no one was visible as we moved down the beach, and no sound that could be at all mistaken for human greeted us. Animals, yes. Birds chirped and iguanas scrambled for cover at our approach, and there was another noise somewhere in the distance I couldn't put a name to. But no talking or laughing or music. None of the sounds you'd typically associate with a resort.

"It's all so eerie," I said, hugging myself against the uneasy feeling that seemed to grow with each passing second.

Boone only nodded

The warm ocean breeze swept over me, lifting my hair. The small building turned up nothing of importance, so we kept moving, reaching an open-air restaurant that was surrounded by pools, which we paused to investigate. The restaurant was stocked with food and drinks and the electricity was still working— Boone informed me that there were solar panels on the island—but still, there were no people.

"You said no one lives here?" I asked as we started walking again.

"Only on and off," Boone said. "Richard Branson has a private home here and he has staff, but maybe he got stuck somewhere else when things got bad. Maybe his staff stayed home with their families."

Just then we rounded a bend, and the sparkling water of a pool came into view, as well as a rather luxurious beach house. Seeing it sitting there made me think about the solar panels and the possibility of still having power when no one else did. A sense of hope surged through me, but even so, I wasn't ready to completely accept that getting home was impossible. Still, this could be a possible temporary solution like Boone suggested.

"We could make this work, you know?" I said, waving toward the building. "Until help comes, I mean."

Boone nodded, but he didn't look all that hopeful. "I mean, there's solar, which is good, but I don't exactly know how to run it."

"We could try." I grabbed his hand, forcing him to stop. "We have to. Don't you think?"

He looked past me to the house, which was still a good ten feet away, and I followed his gaze. There were two tennis courts, one behind the building and one beside it. It was also pretty obvious that the building was more of place to hang out than to sleep. Both floors were open, allowing for breathtaking views but not exactly suitable for living, and there were couches under awnings and tables inside.

I turned back to Boone. "This doesn't look like it has rooms."

"They must be somewhere else on the island." He grabbed my hand and started walking again. "We may be able to find a vehicle here, though."

Like all the other buildings, the beach house was deserted when we finally reached it. Boone had been right, though, and just past the building, two golf carts sat.

Boon sighed in relief when we reached them. "The keys are in the ignition."

"That seems strange," I said, looking around as if expecting someone to appear.

Boone got behind the wheel and I hurried to the other side.

"Maybe whoever drove them last was in a hurry

for some reason." He turned the key and the engine started. "Either way, I'm glad. It will make exploring the island easier."

He turned the golf cart around and pulled onto the road, and I glanced toward the second vehicle as we passed it, curious if it, too, had a key. My heart nearly stopped at the sight of red smeared across the off-white leather seat. Had it been blood? We were past it too quickly for me to know for sure.

"Boone," I put my hand on his leg as I craned my neck, trying to get another look, "I think there was blood in that golf cart."

It was too far away to see.

"What?" He shook his head. "I didn't see anything."

Maybe I'd imagine it.

I gnawed on my lip as I looked around, searching for anything that would indicate something bad had happened here, but the place looked deserted.

Boone slowed to a stop when we reached an intersection. A sign told us that going left would take us to The Great House, while a right turn would lead us to several other structures. Since their names were totally unfamiliar to me, I wasn't sure if they were lodging, but I had a good feeling about place called The Great House, so I pointed that way.

"There."

"You sure?" he asked, looking uncertain.

"No, but it's called a house, so it's worth a try."

"Can't argue with that," he said, and started driving again.

We passed the tennis court at the back of the beach house and came to a curve in the road, and several large animal enclosures came into view. Boone slowed to a stop beside them, giving me a chance to study them. They looked like something you'd find at a zoo, which seemed strange. Even crazier was the fact that all the doors were open and there were no animals in sight.

I had a flashback of random celebrities who'd had large cats as pets. Mike Tyson, who'd owned a tiger was the most memorable, but I'd recently watched a documentary about Tippi Hedren, actress and mother of Melanie Griffith, who'd had a lion as part of her family for years.

These enclosures looked much too small to have housed an animal so large, but something must have lived here. Was it dangerous? Was it loose on the island now?

"What were these for?" I asked Boone, hoping he knew.

"Lemurs, I think," was his instant reply. "I heard Richard Branson was trying to preserve the species. Someone must have let them out when they realized how bad things were."

The ringed tails and big eyes of the adorable primates flashed through my mind, instantly putting me at ease. Thank God it wasn't anything that could rip us apart.

"It's a good thing they were released," I said as Boone once again started driving, "otherwise they might have starved."

"Yeah," he agreed.

We drove on, passing a lake to our right and getting glimpses of the crystal blue Caribbean Sea to our left. It wasn't long before a thatched roof came into view. Boone followed the signs, taking the road up a small hill until at last we found ourselves in front of the house, which was more of a mansion, really. He parked outside and for a moment we stared up at it. After the fear and death and horror of the last two weeks, it seemed totally surreal to be sitting in front of this amazing house. And just in time, too. The sun was getting low and would soon be setting, and after the long day of work, I was more than ready for sleep.

As if reading my mind, Boone climbed out of the golf cart. "It's getting late, so we should just stay here for the night. Assuming no one's around to kick us out, that is. We can check the rest of the island tomorrow."

The house was even more amazing than I could have imagined. With windows everywhere, you could see straight out to the ocean on the main floor. There was a huge dining room table, a bar, multiple sofas and even a pool table. A wraparound porch had hammocks as well as the longest table I'd ever seen, and everywhere I looked was blue.

"This is insane," I said as Boone and I moved about the room.

"And so is the price," he replied, then called out, "Hello? Is anyone here?"

We were met by silence.

We explored the house together, moving from luxurious room to luxurious room. Each one seemed better than the last, and they all had a private balcony and huge bathroom. Up and up we climbed until we finally reached the last and largest room. A massive suite with a huge sundeck, complete with a hot tub and even an outdoor bathtub.

I stopped in the middle of the sundeck and turned to face Boone. "Is it possible for a zombie apocalypse to be this luxurious?"

"Apparently on Necker Island it is." He was frowning, though, looking around. "I just worry that someone else might show up."

"What makes you think someone else will?"

"For all the same reasons you think it's a great place to stay. It's not a secret that Richard Branson owned this island and rented out to wealthy people, and anyone who's familiar with the area might reasonably want to come here."

I hadn't thought of that, but he was right. Still, did it matter? Just this one building had enough space for a dozen people. Couldn't we share?

Since I was too exhausted to even think about that, I said, "We can deal with that tomorrow. For now, I want a shower and maybe a dip in the pool. What do you think?"

I was already pulling my sundress over my head as I headed for the door, which instantly distracted Boone.

His hazel eyes lit up, and despite his previously serious expression, he smiled. "I could go for that."

Back on the bottom floor, we went outside. The sun had moved even lower in the sky while we explored the house, and now the horizon was lit up, making the ocean twice as breathtaking. I paused beside the pool to stare at it for a moment, trying to reconcile how this amazing sight could exist in the same world where zombies were real. It seemed impossible.

Not wanting to think about it, I turned to Boone. He was staring at me, and like the night before, heat simmered between us. The day had been so long and exhausting that I hadn't been able to focus on anything but collecting supplies. Now, though, all thoughts turned to him.

"Come here," he said, grabbing my hips and pulling me closer.

His mouth covered mine and I closed my eyes, willing all the horror of the day to fade. It was easy with his arms around me, and when he led me to a lounge chair instead of the pool, I didn't put up a fight.

Still kissing, he eased me down. He was on top of me, his hands moving up my body, pushing my swimsuit top up in the process. He cupped my breasts as we kissed, his body between my legs and moving in the most deliciously torturous way. It was driving me while, as where his thumbs on my nipples.

Disappointment surged through me when he moved his hands from my breasts, but then he was kissing his way down my body as he worked to undo my swimsuit top, his mouth finding my right nipple only a second after he tossed it away. I moaned and threaded my fingers through his hair, obeying when he urged my legs apart. He rubbed me through my swimsuit for a moment, but as if impatient to feel me, pulled the fabric aside. His fingers went to work then, teasing me, making my legs tremble, all the while sucking on my nipples. Taking turns, driving me crazy.

I was close when he stopped what he was doing and stood, and I watched, panting as he slid his swim trunks down. My swimsuit bottom was next, and then he was on me again, kissing me as he slid inside. The movement was slow, as if he wanted to draw it out, and I found myself thrusting my hips up to meet his, wanting him in me now. He held back, though, teasing me until I thought I might scream in frustration.

When he was finally inside me completely, I expected him to move right away. Instead, he kissed me deeply, his tongue exploring my mouth, his teeth nipping at my bottom lip as he rolled his hips. The movement was enough to do me in, and I cried out as I came, my body pulsing. Quivering.

I'd barely come down before he was moving, this time fast and hard, grunting with each thrust. Behind him, the sun was setting, and between the pleasure he was giving me and the beauty of our surroundings, I found the perfect escape from reality. Boone and this place. At that moment, that was all I needed.

Seven

The open concept of the master suite allowed us to sleep comfortably despite the lack of air conditioning, but I was fairly certain that it was Boone's presence at my side that kept the nightmares at bay. I woke wrapped in a thin, soft sheet, his body pressed against mine as the salty ocean air swept through the room, rustling the canopy above my head. The lapping of water against land, rustling of trees, and songs from birds were the only sounds. It was peaceful, which seemed so at odds with what I knew was happening on the nearby islands. *Zombies.* The very thought made me want to check myself into an insane asylum. It couldn't be real. It was impossible. People didn't come back from the dead and try to eat you.

Yet, I knew it was.

At my side, Boone shifted then stretched, drawing my gaze—and focus—to him. He lifted his arms above his head yawned, his eyes still closed, and I took him in. What a magnificent distraction he was. His body sculpted from years of hard work; his skin bronzed from the sun. He was like a Greek god only better because he'd saved me. If I hadn't bumped into him on Virgin Gorda, I'd be stuck there with the dead instead of at this abandoned luxury resort.

At least we thought it was abandoned. We couldn't be positive since we hadn't explored the other buildings yet, but it seemed unlikely that anyone was around.

Boone's gaze captured mine when he opened his eyes, and he smiled. "Morning."

"Morning," I replied, also smiling.

Like I had a moment ago, he took me in, his expression hungry in a way that had nothing to do with food. I was still naked, the sheet pulled up to just below my breasts. My skin heated under his gaze, and my cheeks flushed. Images from the night before came back in a rush that had my blood simmering in seconds.

"You're a sight to wake up to," Boone said, scooting closer to me.

His mouth covered mine, his hand on the back of my head. I threaded my fingers through his hair and kissed him back, not caring about morning breath or the fact that we needed to explore the island and take stock supplies. Only caring about him.

I was on my back in seconds, him on top of me as the kisses deepened. His stubbled beard was like sandpaper against my skin, but I couldn't care. Not with his body moving against mine, not with his hands teasing me and his tongue exploring my mouth.

A shriek unlike anything I'd ever heard before cut through the silence, and like a switch had been flipped, the mood changed in an instant. Boone released me and sat up, his gaze wide, and I bolted to my feet. The hair on my scalp prickled the way it did during a particularly intense part of a horror movie, and my pulse quickened as fight or flight set in. That sound, wherever it had come from, couldn't have been human. But was it a zombie?

"What was that?" Boone asked even though I knew as much as he did.

"I don't know, but we should probably get dressed."

He nodded as he climbed from bed, already scrambling to collect his clothes from the floor where he'd tossed them the night before.

I ran my fingers through my hair, unworking knots and twisting it into a bun so I could get it out of my face, then grabbed my own clothes. Like yesterday, the skimpy swimsuit and dress I pulled on felt inadequate for this world, but I didn't have anything else. Even worse were the flipflops I shoved my feet into. What if

I had to run? I'd kick them off, of course, but bare feet wouldn't be much better for fleeing danger.

Swiping my knife up off the bedside table, I turned to face Boone. Like me, he had the knife he'd taken from the boat gripped in his hand. The weapons seemed so useless in the face of this unknown, but like the shoes on my feet, I didn't have any other options.

"Ready?" he said.

I nodded in reply.

A second shriek sounded as Boone and I hurried from the room, this time louder than the one before. Closer.

Boone grabbed my free hand and hurried toward the stairs.

"It's an animal," he said. "It has to be."

I thought of the empty cages we'd seen the day before and shuddered. "You think it's the lemurs?"

Boone thought the primates had been the inhabitants of those cages, but that didn't stop my mind from racing with the possibilities, jumping from fanged jungle cats to other, bigger primates that would easily be able to rip us to pieces. Hopefully, whatever had once lived in those pens was used to humans.

"It has to be," Boone replied.

Another shriek sounded seconds after we'd reached the first floor, only this time it was followed by others. They were high-pitched and oddly threatening. As if the creatures making the sounds were announcing that they were on the hunt.

Screeches rang through the air, growing in frequency as Boone and I rushed through the main part of the house and outside where we'd left the golf cart the night before. My gaze darted around, searching both high and low, taking in the nearby trees and tropical forest, but finding nothing. Still, I had the distinct feeling that we were being watched, and it had me on edge.

"Where are they?" I asked, having to raise my voice to be heard over the noise.

The shrieks went on, and then it seemed as if the jungle was coming alive. The nearby trees began to shake, the rattling of their leaves and branches joining the chorus of inhuman screams. Here and there, a tuft of hair was visible as the foliage shifted, but it was always gone too fast for me to be able to make out what it belonged to. It had to be the lemurs, but there was something about the sound they were making that made me wonder if there was some other, inhuman creature stalking us. Their cries sounded so off. So wrong.

"Maybe we should get out of here," Boone said as if reading my mind.

I opened my mouth to respond just as a furry body appeared, emerging from the branches high above our heads. It had a ringed tail and white face, with a black nose and eyes that were also rimmed in black. Like the sound it made when it opened its mouth, there was something about its eyes that didn't seem right. I wasn't an expert on primates by any means, but I'd seen lemurs before, both in pictures and in zoos, and I didn't remember their eyes being so milky.

"What the hell?" Boone muttered, taking a step back.

Images from the dead we'd encountered came rushing back, and my blood ran cold. The few zombies we'd seen had milky eyes just like this. But what did that mean? Could the lemurs have contracted the virus that wiped out most of the human population? No. That didn't make sense. There couldn't possibly be zombie primates. Could there?

The shrieks went on as more and more lemurs emerged from their hiding places. Some were brown and some black and white, while others had ringed tails. No matter the differences in their fur colors, they all had the same milky eyes and let out identical screams, and not a single one looked friendly.

"We have to go," Boone said, pulling me toward the nearby golf cart.

I didn't argue, and I didn't look away from the creatures looming over us as I allowed him to lead me in the right direction. My heart was pounding when I climbed in through the driver's side and scooted across the seat, and it doubled in speed when the first lemur jumped to the ground. The thing stared at us with its hazy eyes and scooted in our direction. Like the human zombies we'd seen, its gait was awkward and lumbering, but its focus was singular.

Boone had the golf cart started in seconds. I grabbed the bar at my side with my free hand and held on as he put the vehicle in reverse, watching as more lemurs leapt from the trees. They were moving toward us, slow but steady, their teeth bared, their cries threatening.

"We're going to pass them on your side!" Boone called, raising his voice to be heard. "Be ready."

There was no point in wishing I was the one behind the wheel since nothing could be done at this point, so instead, I tightened my grip on the knife. I was still holding onto the bar with my other hand, but I knew I might have to release it to defend myself. I just prayed I didn't fall out because I had a feeling that if I did, the lemurs would rip me to shreds.

The golf cart thumped down the road, getting closer to the primates rushing our way. Boone had the gas pedal pressed to the floor, but we were still going slower than I would have liked. Especially considering the dozens of lemurs now moving toward us.

They began to leap in our direction as we drew closer. The first one slammed into the front of the golf cart, letting out a howl of frustration when its body bounced off it. Our tires rolled over the discarded primate, and the crunch of bone seemed to vibrate through me. I wanted to close my eyes against the sound, but I knew I couldn't afford it and instead kept my focus on the animals.

Another one jumped and ricocheted off the side. A third hit the windshield. The fourth had better aim or luck, however, and came flying at me. Claws out, mouth open. Teeth bloody. On instinct, I lifted my knife, the blade pointed straight out since I had no chance to aim. The small furry body made impact with the knife and the creature let out a cry that almost made my ears ring as the blade sank in. Blood, thick and black sprayed from the wound, but since I'd gotten the thing in the chest and not the head, the animal didn't stop flailing. It swiped its claws in my direction and bared its teeth and shrieked until I finally lost my grip on the knife. Both it and the zombie lemur fell, thankfully taking several other primates down in the process.

"I lost my knife!" I screamed, my gaze darting from the still advancing lemurs as we sped past them to Boone.

He was driving like a maniac, swerving to hit the animals, his hands gripping the steering wheel like he wanted to punish it for the predicament we now found ourselves in.

"Take mine." He nodded to the knife tucked into the cup holder between us.

I yanked it free and turned to face the zombies once again, but we'd left most in our dust by that point. The few still coming from the jungle were too far away to reach us. They were still all coming after us, though, dozens of them scampering down the road in a desperate attempt to get us.

"They're following!" I cried out, my eyes wide as I watched the horror trailing after us.

"We'll have to be fast once we reach the boat."

I thought about what that would entail. Untying the lines, pushing off the dock, getting the engine going so we could motor far enough away from the island that we'd be safe. The distance between us and the zombie lemur horde was growing by the second, but I still couldn't imagine we'd have enough time to do all that before they caught up. Then what? Would we be able to fight them off? No, not we. *Me.* I would have to hold them off while Boone got the boat started because he was the only one who knew how to drive it. Could I do it?

Yes. I would because I had to. It was the only option. Just like learning to help with the boat had been the only option when things got bad. I would rise to the challenge. It was that or death.

It was a short drive to the dock, and within minutes our boat had come into view. The lemurs were no longer in sight, but their shrieks hadn't stopped, telling me they were still in pursuit. Boone slammed on the brakes, and I scrambled out of the golf cart. He didn't bother cutting the engine before following me, and together, we took off.

The Lemurs came into view just as we made it to the dock, making my heart jump to my throat. I pumped my legs harder, kept my focus on our goal. When their footsteps thudded against wood, I knew they'd reached the dock. I told myself not to look back, but I couldn't stop myself. Glancing over my shoulder, I nearly screamed at the sight of the dozens of zombie primates hot on our trail.

They chased us as we ran down the dock. Like I'd thought, my flip flops were a hinderance, and I only made it halfway to the boat before kicking them off. One went flying, landing I didn't know where, while the other splashed into the water and sank from sight. I didn't care. I just wanted to get out of here.

"You take care of the line at the bow," Boone called when we reached the boat. "I'll get the stern."

I was panting when I reached the boat, my hair in my face and getting in my way. There was no time to bother with it, though, and I went by feel alone, unwinding the rope from the cleat and tossing it aboard. At the stern, Boone did the same, then waved for me to join him. He hadn't needed to, though, because I was already running his way.

The lemurs were halfway down the dock by the time we made it onto the boat. Their cries were deafening by that point, and I desperately wanted to cover my ears. Instead, I ran to the front bow and grabbed the boathook.

"Push!" Boone called as he climbed the steps to the helm.

He didn't need to tell me twice.

Using the boathook, I pushed us away from the dock just as the lemurs continued their pursuit. The sound of their claws scraping against the wood was somehow audible over their cries, adding to my panic. To make matters worse, the tide seemed determined to keep us next to the dock, and no matter how hard I pushed, the boat wouldn't budge.

My heart thudding violently, I shoved harder, my gaze moving from the boathook to the advancing zombie animals. Their teeth looked doubly sharp, and their shrieks sounded twice as threatening, and every thud of their feet against the dock had the dread inside me building.

I wanted to jump up and down for joy when the engine rumbled to life. Instead, I planted my feet, preparing myself for the boat's movement as I kept my focus on the lemurs. Slowly, we moved away from the dock, putting more distance between us and the creatures, but it was too late.

A brown lemur leapt at me, and I swung the boathook, sending it flying back. It hit the horde behind it, and several went down, but the one closest to me was already in the air. Again, I hit it with the boathook, and again it went flying. I did it with a third one and fourth one, crying out from the impact each time the boathook hit one of the furry zombies.

Finally, we were far enough away from the dock that when the next lemur leapt, it missed and splashed into the water. Panting, I stumbled back, the boathook falling from my hand and dropping to the deck with a thud. Trying to catch my breath, I watched as the horror on the dock went on. Lemurs jumped, too stupid to realize they couldn't reach us, and splashed into the water. They flailed, struggling to stay afloat, but eventually disappeared from sight as more dropped into the ocean at their backs.

As if finally understanding that they wouldn't be able to get us no matter what they did, they stopped jumping after only a minute, but didn't go back to land. Instead, they paced, still shrieking. Still focused on us even though we were well out to sea by that point.

Once I'd calmed down, I turned to face Boone. Our eyes met and for a moment neither one of us moved or blinked or even breathed. We just stared at each other as we tried to wrap our brains around what had just happened.

Finally, he let out a big sigh and the spell was broken. "That was—"

He shook his head like he couldn't think of anything to say.

"Insane?" I offered.

"Yeah." Again, he blew out a breath. "You think all animals were affected by the virus?"

I thought about the few animals we'd seen. The chickens on Virgin Gorda had been fine, and I'd heard a dog barking more than once. Even though I hadn't seen it, the sound hadn't caused the same foreboding the lemurs' shrieks had. As soon as I'd heard those noises, I'd known something was wrong. I also remembered reading an article some time back about chimpanzees contracting human viruses.

"Maybe it's just primates," I suggested.

"None of the other islands in the area have monkeys," he said, "so if that's the case, we should be good."

I felt like crossing my fingers.

Instead, I turned my gaze to the ocean, scanning the nearby islands. "Where to now?"

Silence followed the question, which forced me to focus on Boone. Like me, he was studying our surroundings, taking in the clear blue water and mountainous islands.

"What's our goal?" he said, still not looking at

me.

"To survive," I replied.

"Yeah, I know that." He turned his hazel eyes on me. "But what else? What do we want to focus on?"

I thought about it. Home should have been my answer. I needed to get home. That was a long shot, though. Between the zombies and lack of electricity, trying to sail from the Virgin Islands to the mainland right now just wasn't feasible. Which meant we needed to wait until things got back to normal—or at least as close to normal as possible. What then? What did we need to do now? Survive, yes, but also find a safe place and other people. We needed to build a new kind of normal that would get us through.

"We need to create a life," I told him.

He lifted his eyebrows questioningly. "A life?"

"Yes," I replied. "We need a place to call home. A place to build something that will sustain us after the food is gone."

"A life," he repeated, nodding. "Okay."

"Which island has the smallest population?" I asked.

"Well, there are several islands that are completely inhabited and others that have only resorts, but there's a reason for that. Plus, it would mean starting from scratch. What we need is a sparsely populated island that already has buildings." The corner of his mouth turned up as he nodded, deepening the dimple in his left cheek. "Anegada."

"Anegada?" I shook my head. "I haven't been there."

"It's the only island in the area that isn't volcanic, so unlike the others, it's flat." Boone went on, "Less than three hundred people live on the island, plus there's a huge population of feral cows, donkeys, goats, and even sheep. Meaning we'd have meat."

I perked up at that. "Where would we stay?"

"There are a few resorts. The Anegada Beach Club and the one at Cow Wreck Beach are on the north side of the island. Either would be good since the coral reef helps protect that side of the island from flooding when a big storm does hit."

"And you think going there would be a good idea?"

He shrugged even as he nodded. "I think it could work. At least temporarily."

I blew out a long breath, thinking it through. We hadn't run into many zombies on Virgin Gorda, but that didn't mean they weren't there. I knew the population of that island wasn't huge, but there had definitely been way more than three hundred people living there. Plus, Boone was familiar with the area, and if he thought Anegada was the way to go, I had to trust him.

Before I agreed, though, I had one question.

"No monkeys?"

He laughed, but the sound was tense and awkward. As if he was still shaken by what we'd just gone through.

"No monkeys."

"Okay," I said. "Let's do it."

He grinned and turned the wheel. "Anegada, here we come."

I hoped it was the right decision.

Eight

Sailing to Anegada was different than any of the other trips I'd taken since arriving in the British Virgin Islands. Not only did it take longer, but for much of the trip, it looked as if we were going nowhere. Open sea. That was it. Miles and miles of open sea.

"You sure we're going the right way?" I asked Boone as I squinted toward the horizon and still saw no sigh of the island we were supposedly sailing toward.

He shot me a crooked grin. "I promise."

Since he was the one who knew what he was doing, I decided to take his word for it even if I wasn't completely convinced.

I sat beside him at the helm, the canopy over us blocking out the bright Caribbean sun as the two hulls of the boat cut through the water. We'd put up the mainsail as well as the jib, and thanks to the windy day, we were going a solid seventeen knots. It was slower than if we'd decided to motor, but since it saved us fuel, it was worth it.

The minutes passed and finally a shape began to emerge on the horizon. It was small and barely discernable, but I knew what it was.

I got to my feet and pointed. "Land."

"I told you." He winked. "You need to put more faith in me."

"I have tons of faith in you," I said with a shrug. "I'm just a naturally skeptical person."

"Fair enough," he replied, his focus on the instruments in front of him.

He was frowning, staring at the navigation screen, which showed how deep the water surrounding the island was in metres.

I stood so I could look it over, too, curious if there

was an issue.

As if reading my mind, Boone pointed to the screen. "We need to go in through here because there are a lot of submerged coral heads." He moved his finger to indicate another area. "This is Horseshoe Reef, which is one of the largest barrier coral reefs in the Caribbean. It's caused hundreds of shipwrecks."

My heart jumped to my throat. "Shipwrecks?"

"Don't worry," he said. "Most of those were a long time ago. Before the islands had been properly mapped. Entry into Setting Point is clearly marked now." He finally looked up. "Plus, I've been here more times than I can count."

I relaxed. "Oh. Good."

Boone lifted his hand to shield his eyes as he stared out over the water, and I followed his gaze. We could see more of Anegada now. A handful of boats bobbing on the water, most of them smaller than ours, telling me that few tourists were here. To the right of that was a long building with a blue roof that I could only assume was a hotel of some kind, and a sprinkling of other buildings around it.

Boone pointed past them. "Most of the island's inhabitants live over that way. In The Settlement." He shifted so he was pointing to our left. "The two resorts I mentioned are that way, on the other side of the island. We'll have to drive but finding a car shouldn't be a problem. Tourists can rent one for the day so they can get around the island more easily."

"How big is Anegada?" I asked as I scanned it, realizing it was much larger than I'd expected. With fewer than three hundred full time residents, I'd expected it to be tiny.

"Fifteen square miles or so," he replied. "Not huge, but too big to travel on foot."

We lapsed into silence as we drew closer to the island. I could see the channel markers now, the green ones that were closer to the island and the red ones nearer to us. After two weeks on the boat, I knew we needed to pass between them in order to make it into the bay safely.

"We should put the sails down," Boone said only a few minutes later.

Since the boat was so large, both sails were operated by power winch, making lowering them a snap. After that, all we had to do was secure the sheets to make sure the wind didn't catch the sails and pull them back out, which I did while Boone powered up the motor.

I scanned the shore while he expertly steered the boat between the channel markers, hoping to see some sign of *life*. There would be zombies—nearly three hundred of them if Boone had his facts straight—but I was hoping to find people as well as animals. At the moment, though, everything was still.

"It's so strange," Boone said as we drew closer to the other boats already moored in the bay, "I'm used to someone coming out to greet us. They do their best to steer tourists to their bar or restaurant."

He shook his head like the lack of salesmanship bugged him, but I knew what he was thinking. It was crazy how much had changed so fast.

When we reached the bay, we worked together to get the boat secured to the mooring ball. Like the other times, it was a snap, and even though I was tense at the thought of what we might face once we reached land, I couldn't help feeling proud as well. I'd learned so much over the last two weeks.

Boone lowered the dinghy while I loaded some supplies into the waterproof bags. I'd lost my knife on Necker Island, but a quick search of the kitchen and I was able to find another one. It was smaller, but better than nothing. Hopefully, we'd be able to pick up something better on land. Within ten minutes of mooring, we were in the dinghy and on our way to land.

I found myself searching for movement as Boone drove. Water splashed me, soaking my dress, but I barely noticed. I was too busy taking in Setters Point. The building with the blue roof turned out to be Anegada Reef Hotel, and there were a few restaurants and bars, as well as signs for gifts shops. A place to rent cars. A bakery. A sign for a grocery store.

No people, and as far as I could tell, no zombies.

We tied off on a small dock and Boone climbed out before turning to help me. To my left, a wood structure stood in a few feet of clear, blue water, two swings hanging from it. They swayed in the breeze as if controlled by phantoms, and something about it had a shiver moving down my spine. Or maybe it was the utter stillness of the island that did it. Either way, I felt certain I would have nightmares tonight.

"Hello?" Boone called.

My back stiffened as I prepared for a zombie to come running, but we were met by silence. Even so, I clung tightly to my knife.

"Where to?" I asked when Boone remained silent a beat too long for my taste.

He sighed and nodded to our right. "This way."

Barefoot and desperately wishing for shoes when a sharp shell or rock poked my sole, I followed him past the hotel and bar built right on the sand. Just beyond it we came to a squat building painted yellow that had a handful of vehicles parked beside it. They looked similar to Jeeps, with a black canvas top and no doors, but the word MOKE was above the grill in silver letters.

I paused in front of a bright red one. "Moke?"

"They're electric," Boone said, "so unless they're charged, we're better of getting one of those."

He nodded to a faded blue Suzuki that didn't look nearly as festive as the other vehicles but made me feel a hell of a lot more secure because it had doors. If zombies did attack, I wanted to be able to lock myself inside.

"I like it," I said with a nod.

Boone was already at the front door of the

building, which apparently wasn't locked because it opened without issue. He frowned with it only cracked an inch, then tightened his grip on his knife and looked my way.

"Be ready in case the owner is still here."

And not human were the unspoken words.

Bracing myself, I held my knife out in front of me as if preparing to spear a charging zombie. Satisfied that I was prepared, Boone pulled the door open the rest of the way, his own knife up and ready, and waited. When nothing happened, he poked his head inside.

"It's clear," he called a second later. "I'll grab the keys. Be right back."

The island was utterly silent, but since I was myself with so much unknown out there, I found myself looking around, anyway. The last thing I wanted was to get caught off guard.

The wind blew, lifting my skirt, and a few tendrils of hair escaped from the bun I'd hastily made that morning. They tickled my nose, so I tucked them behind my ear, but more broke free with the next breeze. I didn't bother with those, however, because I was too focused on the stench of death that slammed into me.

My heart thudding harder, I spun around, scanning everything as I did. Something nearby was dead, but where was it? I saw nothing, so I kept spinning in a circle, not wanting whatever it was to sneak up on me. There were buildings all around me, though, and nothing moving but the trees. Seconds passed and the stink didn't go away, but nothing appeared. It was possible that whatever I was smelling was just a dead person and not a zombie and I knew it, but I couldn't force my heart to stop thudding. Especially not after our close call with the lemurs.

"Where are you?" I murmured.

Seconds later, a moan made the hair on my arms stand on end. I spun toward the sound just as a zombie stumbled from between two buildings, headed my way. It was a woman, her once dark brown skin now an ashy gray color, her bright blue shorts and white shirt ripped and stained. She had her arms up, reaching, and her head was cocked slightly to the side as her milky eyes focused on me. Fingers grasped at air; teeth chomped. My heart beat harder, nearly drowning out her moans.

Desperately, I looked toward the building Boone had disappeared into. Where was he? Nearly five minutes had passed, which should have been more than enough time to locate the keys. Yet he still hadn't reappeared.

The zombie moaned again, pulling my attention to her. She was ten feet from me now, and I knew that even if Boone stepped out of the building at this very moment, he wouldn't make it to me. I was going to have to take care of myself if I wanted to make it through this.

Planting my feet, I took a deep breath and adjusted my hold on the knife. My palm was damp with sweat, but there was no time to do anything about it, so instead, I simply curled my fingers tighter. She was six feet from me now, two more steps and I'd be within arm's reach of her. There was no time to waste.

After taking a moment to consider the situation, I decided that even though I wasn't wearing any shoes, the best course of action was to go for her leg. Ducking so I was beneath her arms, I stuck my foot out and hooked it around the back of her ankle, then pulled my leg forward. She stumbled, toppled backward, and slammed into the ground, giving me the chance I needed. I pounced, landing on top of her on my knees, gasping. The stink of rot filled my nostrils, making me gag, and I had to swallow down bile. There was no time to throw up, not with her flailing beneath me. Striking, I brought my knife down, slamming the blade through her milky eye and into her brain. The impact was jarring, vibrating through me, and the sickening squelch of the knife cutting through tissue and brain matter made my already uneasy stomach lurch, but she stopped moving. Which allowed me to turn my head when the contents of my stomach jumped to my throat.

I was heaving when Boone called out, "Moira!"

My back was to him, so I held my hand out as I wretched again, not wanting him to come any closer. The contents of my stomach splashed to the ground, spattering my dress and the body next to me. I heaved again; my eyes closed this time, so I didn't have to see my vomit hitting the rotting body that had just tried to eat me.

When I was finally done, I sat back and wiped my mouth, but didn't open my eyes. I wanted to make sure the nausea didn't come back, because even though my stomach was empty now, that didn't mean I couldn't dry heave.

"Moira?" Boone said after a second.

I opened my eyes to find him standing over me, a concerned expression on his face.

"I'm okay." I climbed to my feet and headed for the beach, which was less than twenty feet away. "I just need to clean up."

He didn't say anything, but the footsteps at my back told me he was following.

I waded into the water, pulling my filthy dress over my head as I did. Once I was in up to my thighs, I sank to my knees, dipping the dress under at the same time. I held it under with one hand while scooping up a handful of ocean water with the other, which I slurped up but didn't swallow. I swished it around and gargled, the salt a welcome break from the taste of vomit, then spit it out. Another handful of water was used to wash my face, and then I was standing, wringing my dress out, and holding it up to make sure it was clean. Once I was sure, I turned back to face Boone.

"You okay?" he asked.

"I'll be fine." I continued to wring out my dress as I waded toward him. "I mean, who hasn't vomited after killing an undead woman? It's just par for the course, right?"

He let out an unamused snort. "Unfortunately, I don't think you're far off."

I rolled my eyes and mimicked his humorless laugh. "You get the keys?"

He held them up.

"Good." I started walking, heading toward the waiting Suzuki. "Let's get out of here. I need some new clothes."

I still had the soaking dress in my hand when I climbed into the car, and I tossed into the back seat even though I didn't know why. Hopefully, I could find something more practical at one of the resorts. Someone had to have left clothes behind.

We drove in silence. The roads were pitted with holes but decent enough, and we passed few buildings once we'd gotten away from Setters Point. Boone seemed to know which way to go and navigated the island with no issue despite the lack of signs. After about five minutes, I leaned over and peered at the gas gauge, curious how much was in the tank. The needle was slightly below the F. With only fifteen square miles to explore, we would be good for a while.

We saw no zombies and no people, but Boone did slow to a stop when we spotted a Donkey. It more than thirty feet away, surrounded by bushes and brambles, and seemed healthy enough. It was too thin, but it wasn't charging toward us with its big, square teeth bared, so that was a good sign.

"It looks okay," Boone said, echoing my thoughts.

"Yeah." I scanned the area, expecting to see other hooved animals, but spotted none. "How many feral animals did you say lived on this island?"

He started driving. "Hundreds. Maybe over a thousand. More than there were people."

I turned to face him. "Hundreds?"

"Yup."

I turned my attention back to the landscape, but once again there was nothing. I couldn't imagine hundreds of feral animals being able to hide from view for long. Although, figuring out how to kill them was going to be a challenge. It wasn't like our little kitchen knives would do the trick.

A sign for Anegada Beach Club came into view, and Boone took a right. As if from out of nowhere, thatched roofs appeared, and less than a minute later, he pulled to a stop outside a gift shop and put the Suzuki in park. More thatched roofs were visible beyond it, as well as a small pool and a bar with a thatched roof. There were a couple other cars—two Mokes as well as a truck—but like every other place we'd been, no people.

We climbed out and paused to look around.

"What do you think?" he asked.

"I think it's going to be as deserted as every other place, but I'd love to search the rooms and maybe find some better clothes." I waved my bare right foot at him. "And shoes."

"We'll see what we can find," he said, already heading for the gift shop.

It yielded nothing. Overpriced t-shirts that didn't really help when it came to preparing for zombies and miscellaneous items like Christmas ornaments with *Anegada* printed on them. I pulled on a t-shirt in case I was unable to find anything else, but hoped it was only a temporary solution. Long sleeves were preferable.

From there we headed to the hotel, passing the pool and bar. A sand volleyball court was visible in the distance, and beyond that what appeared to be little huts dotted the dunes. I counted nine of them, and between those and the sixteen rooms in the main hotel building, I knew it wouldn't take long to search them all. I was hoping at least one person had been stranded here when things got bad and left some clothes behind. I was also hoping that unless they were still alive, we didn't run into them.

Like the gift shop, the hotel was a dead end, and the huts—which ended up being a lot more luxurious than I had imagined--were the same. Apparently, everyone had evacuated when travel was cut off weeks ago.

Back at the pool area, Boone ducked behind the bar so he could pour us some drinks. "There are a few other resorts we can check out, plus The Settlement."

"That's something," I said.

He knelt to get something off a shelf and paused. "The fridge is on."

"Really?" I lifted myself on my tiptoes so I could look over the bar just as he stood and opened the ice maker.

Cool air rushed out, nearly making me sigh, and the sight of the little cubes of ice was probably one of the most beautiful things I'd ever seen.

"The power is on," Boone said, confusion coating the statement.

"You think they have a generator?" I asked.

He looked around, frowning. "Maybe. Or it could be that the power hasn't gone out on the island yet. They're so far away from the other islands that they have to have their own powerplant."

I thought about what that could mean for us if we chose to stay here. Electricity. It was one of the things that had drawn us to Necker Island, but the lemurs had ruined that plan. If Anegada had its own powerplant, though, we might be able to keep it working. The only way to find out for sure was to explore the rest of the island.

Boone slid a glass across the counter, and still reeling from the possibilities, I happily took it. While getting trashed when we had no clue what was going to happen next wasn't a good idea, I felt like I deserved a drink after taking out a zombie completely by myself then vomiting all over the poor dead woman.

I took a swig, wincing at the heavy pour of vodka, swallowed, and took a second one. It went down easier.

"Where to next, then?" I asked.

"Cow Wreck Beach," Boone replied after taking

a sip of his own drink.

"Cow Wreck Beach?" I repeated doubtfully. "That's strange name."

"In the 1920s, a steel freighter full of cow bones hit the reef and sank."

This time, I actually balked. "Cow bones?"

"They were going to be turned into fertilizer or something." Boone shrugged as he took another drink. "Anyway, it hit one of those reefs famous for shipwrecks and that was the end of that. I guess you can still find cow bones on the ocean floor."

I shuddered at the thought. "I'll take your word for it."

Boone smiled, threw the rest of his drink back, and nodded to my half-empty glass. "You ready to check it out? If nothing else, it's a beautiful beach."

"Yeah." I chugged my own drink and set it down, shaking my head as if trying to get rid of the fogginess in my brain left behind by the vodka. It didn't work.

Maybe one drink had been one drink too many…

Nine

A handful of small houses painted in bright shades of orange, aqua, yellow, green, and pink were the first things we came upon when we reached Cow Wreck Beach. Beyond that a few other buildings stood. An open-air bar and restaurant, a few buildings that seemed to be used for storage, as well as a gift shop, which I would be hitting up very soon in addition to exploring the villas.

First, though, Boone and I went to the bar to see if it had electricity.

"Well?" I asked as he opened the fridge.

"It's working."

"Either both places have a generator, or you were right, and the island has its own power."

"We'll have to explore more places to know for sure," he said, coming around the bar to join me.

"Yeah," I murmured as I looked around, taking in my surroundings. Considering the possibilities.

The bar overlooked the beach, and even though I should have been thinking about the electricity, all I could focus on as I stared at the never-ending ocean was that Boone had been right about Cow Wreck Beach. It was breathtaking.

He and I stood side by side, watching the calm aquamarine water lap at the white sand beach as palm fronds swayed above our heads. Farther out, the coral heads Boone had told had me about were visible through the crystal ocean and the ocean stretched on for miles and miles. Nothing else was in sight, but instead of making me feel lost, it was a relief to be so secluded.

"We could start a life here," he said.

I turned to face him. "Here?"

I looked around, taking in the guest houses, the

restaurant and stocked bar, and the beauty of the whole place. I had to admit it was one of the most gorgeous places I'd ever been, but we were so cut off. And what would we do if a hurricane hit?

"We can at least give it a shot," Boone said. "If it doesn't work out, we have the boat. I just think it would be better than trying to make a go of it on one of the more populated islands. The zombies, you know?"

I shuddered and hugged myself, remembering my encounter with the dead woman just a short time ago. "Yeah. Maybe."

"We can start gathering supplies," Boone went on, as if I'd already agreed. "Go from resort to resort, then from house to house. Bring it all here."

My gaze swept across the area again, taking it all in. Imagining Boone and me building something here. Even if the power went out, it could work. Plus, he was right. If we decided it wasn't the right place, we had the boat.

Still, there was a part of me that felt like settling this far away was admitting I'd never make it home. Even though I'd been trying to accept that fact, the thought still twisted my stomach into knots. Most of my family was gone for sure. I knew that because I'd heard the defeat in my mom's voice. Going home wouldn't change that. But I still wanted to believe that somehow, someday, I would make it back.

For the meantime, though, I knew I needed to try and build something here.

"Let's give it a shot," I said, meeting Boone's gaze. Forcing out a smile.

He grinned, a genuine smile that nearly lit me on fire, and grabbed me, pulling me against him so he could cover my mouth with his. The kiss was hot enough to melt away some of trepidation, and the rest evaporated the second his hand cupped my breast. I stood on my tiptoes, wanting to be closer to him as the kiss deepened. His hand moved from my breast, traveling down my stomach before moving back up.

This time under my stolen t-shirt. My swimsuit top offered no resistance when he tugged it aside, and I moaned into his mouth when his thumb grazed my nipple.

The kisses and caresses continued as we collapsed on the ground beneath a palm tree. I'd never made love on the sand before, and even though the rough particles were scratchy and irritating, I had no desire to stop long enough to find a better place. My shirt was yanked over my head, the other triangle of my top was pulled aside, and then Boone was tugging at my swimsuit bottoms. They were off in seconds, and then he squirmed out of his before positioning himself between my legs. He entered me without preamble, making me cry out. His thrusts were hard and fast, his face buried in my neck as I clung to him, my nails digging into his back.

The sex was fast and frantic, and over seconds after I cried out my release. My eyes were squeezed shut when Boone thrust into me one final time and grunted. Seconds later, he rolled off me, and we lay side by side on the beach as we worked to catch our breath. I had sand in every crevice, and it wasn't the least bit pleasant, but the pleasure thrumming through me made it impossible to care. In fact, with Boone lying naked at my side, I found it hard to care about anything else. He was the perfect distraction from this world, but I suddenly realized he was something else as well. He was my chance to move on. For two years I'd been licking my wounds and letting life go by, and it had been such a waste. So stupid. So childish. Now, the world I knew was gone, but I had an opportunity to find myself and create something, and I was going to take it. It wouldn't be what I'd dreamed, but that didn't mean we couldn't make it good.

Boone rolled over to face me. "We should get cleaned up, so we can get to work."

"Yeah," I said, but didn't move.

Instead, I stared at him, holding his gaze. Picturing

the future we were going to build together. Thinking about Boone and me. About everything we could do. Together.

"What is it?" he asked.

His stubbled cheek scratched at my palm when I put my hand on his face. "I'm glad I met you."

His expression softened. "Me too."

We cleaned off in the ocean, which left my skin sticky and raw, but I had a feeling it was a sensation I was going to have to get used to. The power was on still, but we didn't yet know how long it would last and we needed to conserve energy. Which meant using the ocean as much as possible. At least until we were more certain of our situation.

After pilfering some clothes—and boat shoes—from the small gift shop, Boone and I took some time to explore the villas. They were small but nice, each one with a full kitchen, a small dining and living area, a bathroom, and one or two bedrooms. Just like the Anegada Beach Club, however, our exploration yielded nothing. It seemed as if all the guests had made it off the island.

It was nearing midday by the time we loaded back into the Suzuki. The sun was bright, the day warm and the sky cloudless. We drove in silence, each of us keeping an eye out. I spotted a couple more hooved animals this time. Another donkey, as well as a goat, but like the first one I'd seen, they were far from the road. Maybe they never ventured close to it.

The animals, although welcome, drew less of my attention than the zombies we passed. The first I spotted off in the distance, stumbling along the beach as if on vacation rather than in search of flesh to devour. Since it was too far away, we had to let it be, but the second one we came upon was in the middle of nowhere, crouched on the side of the road and feasting on a mangled mat of orange, bloody fur.

Boone slowed ten feet away from the creature, which seemed totally unaware of our presence despite the car's humming engine. It was too busy gnawing on its meal, and the sight of the dead thing sinking its teeth into the matted fur of whatever poor animal this had once been turned my stomach.

"We should take care of any we see," Boone said as he pulled his knife from the center console.

He was right. Each zombie we took out meant one less we would have to worry about later.

I gripped my own knife tighter and nodded.

We climbed from the Suzuki at the same time, but I doubted Boone was trembling the way I was. My legs shook and my palms began to sweat, and the tremors only intensified when the zombie looked up from its lunch. Like the woman from earlier, his once dark brown skin was now ashy and had a grayish hue to it, and his eyes were milky when they landed on us. He opened his mouth and let out a moan, revealing bits of bloody flesh stuck between his teeth.

In an instant, his kill was forgotten. It fell from his hands as he stumbled to his feet, already reaching toward us. The man had been a big guy in life, with broad shoulders and meaty arms, and a gut that hung over the waistband of his pants. He had to weigh twice as much as I did and had more than fifty pounds on Boone. Not that he seemed at all intimidated by the zombie's size.

Boone stepped forward, knife raised, and appraised the situation before striking. The zombie was still more than an arm's length away when Boone darted around him, and I held my breath, watching as the creature twisted, trying to keep up. He was too slow, though, and in no time, Boone had grabbed the back of his shirt. He struggled to hold the zombie still, but somehow managed despite the creature's girth and the fact that he was more than a head taller than Boone. A second later, Boone shoved the blade into the side of the zombie's head, right through its ear, and the thing went down. Dead at last.

I let out a deep sigh. "I wish we had a better way

to kill them."

"Maybe we'll get lucky and find a gun in someone's house," Boone said as he headed back to the car. "Or maybe there's a police station."

"That would be nice," I replied, as I once again took a seat on the passenger side.

We continued on, passing the part of the island we'd already seen and once again finding nothing moving around, then moving on to The Settlement.

The houses were small and spread out, the yards a combination of sandy earth and scraggly green plants. Rocks and conch shells had been used to surround gardens where tropical plants sprouted from the ground. We passed a small museum, the Iguana sanctuary, as well as a fire station, but that wasn't all. We also passed a hell of a lot of zombies.

They stumbled from open doors and between houses, drawn out by the sound of our engine. Dozens of them, men and women, children and the elderly. All of them desperate to get us.

Even though we'd been expecting it, the sight of them was jarring after seeing so few. Even worse was the knowledge that we couldn't stop here. Not to search the houses and not to kill any of them. We were too outnumbered.

"You think they remember anything about their lives?" I asked as a zombie woman stumbled from a house, a zombie child only steps behind her.

"What do you mean?"

"Just that. I mean, if they're still hanging around their homes like this, it makes me wonder if they somehow know *this* was where they once lived."

Boone frowned, but I wasn't sure if it was because the thought hadn't occurred to him or if he thought it was far-fetched.

"Maybe there just wasn't any noise to draw them away until now," he said instead of answering my question.

I went back to staring at the zombies as we passed

them.

We made it through The Settlement without any of the dead getting too close to us, and traveled on, passing the only school on the island, as well as another resort called Sea Grape Villas. Since the dead were still trailing after us, stopping to search it for supplies was out of the question, so Boone drove on.

For a while we saw nothing but green plants and sandy dirt, but eventually we made it to the other side of the island and came upon a sign for Loblolly Beach Retreat.

Boone tuned in and a few blue villas came into view, but just like all the other resorts we'd come to since arriving on the island, the area was deserted.

"I'm starting to wonder if we're the only survivors in the whole world," I said when he'd put the car in park.

Boone frowned, but after a second, forced his lips to form a smile. "It could be worse, right? I mean, you're hot. I'm hot. We have amazing sex."

I snorted. "I guess it's about the best scenario you could hope for in a situation like this."

It was a lie and we both knew it.

We climbed out, knives grasped in our hands and ready just in case we came upon any trouble. A blue painted boardwalk led from the bar and restaurant to the gift shop and cottages, which we followed in silence. We stopped at every building we came to, but as expected they were all locked and empty. Like the other resorts, the power was on, but the restaurant looked as if it hadn't been opened in weeks, and the condition of the beach seemed to confirm the fact that no one had been here in some time. Typically, the sand would have been disturbed by footprints, but the tide had smoothed it out, and now it was totally pristine.

Boone blew out a long breath. "There has to be one or two other people on this island at least."

"Why?" I asked, shaking my head. "There were fewer than three hundred people living here when the virus hit. Even if it killed ninety percent of them, the survivors could have been eaten by zombie by now. Let's face it, Boone, we're all that's left."

He shoved his hand through his hair in frustration, shaking his head to indicate he wasn't willing to accept it. I admired his optimism even if I thought it was foolish.

We did what we'd come to do and broke into all the buildings in search of supplies. We raided the Flash of Beauty restaurant and every cottage, as well as the bar and main buildings of the resort, loading everything we found into the Suzuki. It was too small, of course, but thankfully, the resort had a truck on the premises and after a quick search of the main office, we were able to find the right keys. Boone drove it out of the parking lot while I followed him in the Suzuki.

With so few roads on the island, it was virtually impossible to get lost even if I hadn't had Boone to lead me. With the sparkling waters of the Caribbean to my right, I was almost able to convince myself I was on the vacation of my dreams instead of stuck in this nightmare. At least until we came upon a body of water in the center of the island, and I caught sight of a zombie chowing down on a bright pink flamingo.

I drove faster.

With the vehicles loaded down and dusk setting in, we chose to return to our little sanctuary on Cow Wreck Beach rather than raid anything else today. Tomorrow, we could gather more. Now, though, we needed to unload and get some rest.

The cold storage at the restaurant was just big enough to accommodate our new supplies. Once we had them stashed away, Boone poured us two more drinks and we moved to the beach. Sitting in blue Adirondack chairs, we sipped our drinks and watched as the sky slowly changed colors.

We were still sitting there when the sound of engines broke through the silence.

Boone bolted to his feet, his eyes wide with

shock, but I didn't move. I was frozen in place, unsure of what to do and wondering if I was imagining when Boone started moving. The sound of someone calling out a greeting echoed through the night a few seconds later. That snapped me out of it.

My heart thumping, I jumped to my feet and spun to face the bar. Boone was on his way to the parking lot where a truck sat, its engine still running, its lights on, and *people* in the back.

People! Other survivors! My heart leapt at the sight of them.

We weren't alone.

I couldn't believe it, but it got me moving. My hair was a wild mess from the long day of work and the ocean breeze, and I had to push it aside as I jogged after Boone. He was nearly to the truck now, and even though he had his knife in his hand, he seemed relaxed. Which was a good thing, because until this moment, I hadn't considered just how dangerous bumping into other survivors might be.

There were six of them from what I could see, two men in the cab and four more in the back. They ranged in ages from a woman in her early twenties to a guy who looked to be in his sixties. The oldest man was behind the wheel of the truck and seemed to be the one in charge because he and Boone were talking, and I could tell from his accent that he was a local. At least local to the British Virgin Islands. He might not have been from Anegada.

"We been looking for other people. Not having much luck, though." The man waved his hand as if to indicate the rest of the island. "There's nothing out there, man."

He was a thin guy, wiry but fit for his age, with dark skin and a spattering of freckles across his face. His head was covered in gray fuzz and the lines around his mouth and eyes were deep, and although he wasn't large, he had a big presence about him.

"Are you from Anegada?" Boone asked.

"No," the man replied. "Just sailed here today hoping to find other survivors. We been to Tortola and Virgin Gorda."

At his side, a man in his forties with pasty skin and sunburnt cheeks frowned. Of the six people, only he and one other were white, but it only took one quick scan of the group to know that three were tourists like me. The man with pasty skin, a woman who was around my age with a cocoa complexion and big, brown eyes, and a woman around the same age whose bronzed skin had the look of someone who'd spent a lot of time lying in the sun.

The other three were clearly local. There was the older man who'd taken the lead, a girl in her twenties with dark brown skin who had her hair shaved to her scalp, as well as man with a round belly, lighter brown skin, and big, sad eyes. He sat at the back of the group, watching us with a deep frown on his face that gave off the impression it would be a permanent part of him. I caught sight of a gold band on his left hand, and my heart twisted painfully. He'd lost a wife, probably some kids as well.

It made me think of my own family back home, of my nieces and nephews, and for the first time since talking to my mom, I allowed myself to think about what they might have gone through. Did my brother and sister have to watch their children die? I hoped not, although the alternative was even more heartbreaking. What if one or more of the kids had lived while all the adults in my family had died? What if they were alone right now and scared? The thought brought tears to my eyes that I had to blink away.

"I'm Remmy, by the way," the man was saying. He waved to the pasty-faced man at his side. "Pat." Then he jerked his thumb to the people in the back. "Marcus." The big man with sad eyes nodded. "Helen." The local girl shifted her feet. "Deborah and Seneta." He indicated the two tourists—I wasn't sure which was which.

"Good to meet you. I'm Boone," he waved to me, "and this is Moira."

There were a few mumbled hellos, as well as nods in our direction but no one reacted much to meeting us. Remmy, alone, seemed able to focus on what was happening. I wasn't sure if he was just that type of person—the one who could power through no matter what—or if he hadn't lost anything. Either way, the others were lucky to have found him. Or to have been found by him.

Boone tilted his head, his gaze on Remmy. "We spent the day scavenging the Loblolly Resort for supplies. We got a good amount, but it was getting late, so we figured we'd hit some of the other places tomorrow. Luckily, the electricity is still on."

"And it should stay that way as long as we can make it work," Remmy said. "Anegada has its own fossil-fuel-based power station and an ocean water desalination system that will provide us with all the fresh water we need as long as we keep things in running order."

"I was wondering about that," Boone replied with an impressed nod.

"It's one of the reasons I decided to come here," Remmy continued. "The small population was another bonus, then there are the feral animals."

"We saw a few today," Boone told him.

"And zombies?" Remmy asked.

"Most seem to be hanging around their homes," I said, speaking up for the first time.

"The Settlement is pretty overrun," Boone agreed.

"Well," Remmy said thoughtfully, "we'll have to take them out a little at a time, I guess. In the meantime, I figured Cow Wreck was a safe bet. As long as you don't mind sharing."

He said it with note of challenge in his tone. As if he was testing us, wanting to see how open we were to working together.

"It's fine with me." Boone's gaze moved to the

people in the back of the truck. "We were planning to gather as many supplies as we could from other areas, and between that and taking out the dead, we have a lot of work ahead of us. With more hands, we can get it done faster."

"I agree." Remmy finally cut the engine on the truck and climbed out.

As if it was a signal that things were okay, the others did as well, and seeing them standing there did something to me. It gave me hope. I really had thought Boone and I might be alone in this world, but I'd been wrong. There were others, and if we worked together, we just might make it through this thing.

Ten

e worked to clear the island over the next few weeks. It was slow going thanks to the zombies all being congregated in one area, but the work was getting done. All the resorts were cleaned out first, then any buildings not too close to The Settlement. Remmy and Boone made it to the power station and figured out how to work things, and as buildings were cleaned out, we shut power down where it wasn't needed. Pat, it turned out, had been a hunter, and once we found a few pistols at the local police station, he proved to be a huge asset when it came to getting meat. Helen, who had grown up on Tortola, had been the daughter of a fisherman and was more than happy to take over that work, and Seneta had owned a restaurant in the small town in Florida where she used to live and was happy to cook.

The weeks went by, then months. We celebrated Christmas on the beach, the sun beating down on us as we exchanged gifts we'd pilfered from other people's homes. More survivors arrived on the island, many of whom joined us at Cow Wreck Beach while others took up residence at the Anegada Beach club. There were also quite a few that we were forced to run off when they proved they weren't willing to work together.

What had started as a way to distract myself became something so much bigger, and by the time the new year rolled around, I realized I'd fallen in love with Boone. We had a home in a bright pink villa where we slept and made love, and a life that was full of hard work, sunshine, and people who had gone from strangers to family. We laughed together, cried together when we talked about the people we'd lost, and dreamed about the future together. It was uncertain. We had no clue what was going on away from the island, if the zombies were still out there—we'd taken care of all of them on Anegada as far as we knew—if there were other groups of survivors trying to make a new life for themselves just like we were, or if all our hard work would be wiped out by a hurricane. But none of that mattered, because for the time being, we were happy. We'd set out to create a future for ourselves, and we'd succeeded.

A year after arriving in the British Virgin Islands, I found myself lying on the sand next to the man of my dreams. The sky was bright blue and clear, and somewhere in the distance, a bird cawed. Water lapped at my toes, which I wiggled until they had made a home in the sand, and Boone, who had my hand in his, lifted it to his lips. I stared at him as he pressed a soft kiss to my knuckles, awed by how much had changed and more grateful than I could ever put into words.

Behind him, two other people in our group laughed as they descaled a few fish. Helen, who was smiling more and more every day, and Bret, who had arrived on Anegada just a few months ago. He'd been in Tortola this whole time but had come here with a few other people after their group was attacked by a horde of zombies. He'd brought with him fresh supplies we'd desperately needed, but also news about the outside world. The dead still roamed and showed no signs of slowing down, and all semblance of law and order was gone. Gangs of survivors ruled the islands, taking what they needed or just what they wanted, and those who dared stand against them paid with their lives. There was no government, no schools, or hospitals, or first responders. There was nothing but anarchy.

The news had verified that we'd made the right decision in coming here.

We'd destroyed all our docks in hopes of keeping people way, but we knew that couldn't protect us completely. Still, we hoped the people causing havoc on the other islands would keep their distance. That they were satisfied with the chaos there or at the very least thought a trip to our little island wasn't worth their time.

"I love you," Boone whispered, rolling onto his side so he could get closer to me, my hand still clasped in his.

"I love you."

He gave me the smile I'd come to know and love, crooked, his dimple deepening beneath the stubble I'd long ago gotten used to. From time to time, my heart still ached for the family I'd lost, but for the most part, I was content with the life we'd created. A year ago, I hadn't thought I had any happiness in my future, but I'd been wrong.

My gaze moved to my rounded stomach when Boone set his hand on it, and my smile widened until it felt like my cheeks would crack. I was more than happy now. I was overjoyed.

The End

About the Author

Kate L. Mary is an award-winning author of Adult, New Adult, and Young Adult fiction, ranging from post-apocalyptic tales of the undead to Speculative Fiction and Contemporary Romance. Her YA book, *When We Were Human*, was a 2015 Children's Moonbeam Book Awards Silver Medal winner for Young Adult Fantasy/Sci-Fi Fiction, and a 2016 Readers' Favorite Gold Medal winner for Young Adult Science Fiction. Her book *Outliers* was a Top 10 Finalist in the 2018 Author Academy Awards for Sci-Fi/Fantasy Fiction, a Finalist in the 2018 Wishing Shelf Book Awards, and the First Place Winner in the 2018 Kindle Book Awards for Sci-Fi/Fantasy Fiction. Her post-apocalyptic novel, *Tribe of Daughters*, was an Honorable Mention in the 2018 SPR Book Awards, a Bronze Medal Winner in the 2019 Readers' Favorite Book Awards for Science Fiction, and a Semi-Finalist in the 2019 Kindle Book Awards for Sci-Fi/Fantasy Fiction.

You can learn more about Kate L. Mary and her books at www.KateLMary.com